EMBER & FLAME

Bloodlust Book Two

By

J.M. Adele

Ember and Flame

J.M. Adele © 2019

All rights reserved

Edited by CREATING ink
Cover Design by Book Flare Publishers
Cover photo from Deposit Photos © Dmitri Lobanov
Proofed by Fiona Dreaming Proofreading and Formatting
Formatted by Book Flare Publishers

Print Edition

ISBN: 978-0-9944516-8-2

For my Gems who volunteered for the torture of beta reading a cliffhanger. Here is your closure. Thank you!
#sorrynotsorry

Author's Note

If you're reading this before reading *Ashes and Dust*, please stop. You need to read *Ashes and Dust* first. Sorry, but them's the rules. Don't spoil it for yourself.

Check out www.jmadele.com for more information on where to get Ashes & Dust.

If you've read A&D, carry on! Thanks for reading.

Contents

Chapter

One

Polo

Shiloh leapt over the terrain, her ribcage surging for air. Devlin followed closely.

Abandoning the car at the quarry, she hit the road, speeding faster than a blink on the smooth surface. She thought of her time with Seth. The declarations of love. The tender caresses. The stolen moments before dawn.

All lies.

He'd been grooming her, and she'd invited him in.

But why? Why had it taken so long for him to bite?

She wanted to hurl boulders at the earth until a crater formed, a small-scale example of the destruction inside her chest.

That *had* been his voice at the pool before she'd been attacked.

Marco?

Marco?

Marco?

Oh, God. What had he done to Lanie?

They reached the house, finding Lanie's window open. Devlin jumped through first. "She's not here."

Shiloh's mood darkened further, and she lashed out at the nearest target. "Why are you here? I don't need your help."

He ignored her, reaching for the cell phone on the bed.

"Don't touch anything."

The laptop was still open on the desk, its screen lighting up when she tapped the mousepad. Seth's face stared back at her with the details of his description, and where and when he'd last been seen. Nearly two years ago, he'd gone missing from downtown LA. And his real name was Jax.

The closet door was ajar, but that wasn't unusual. The bed was neat. Mostly. There was a creased indent near the foot. *Maybe Lanie sat there during our phone call?* Nothing around the room looked amiss—apart from the gaping window. Lanie didn't like it open.

Seth—no, Jax must've jumped in and snatched her. Lanie wouldn't have even had a chance to scream.

Shiloh sank onto the mattress, her bleak stare aimed outside to the house across the street. He wouldn't have taken her sister there. Too obvious.

"Do ya still feel the pull towards him?"

Her eyes snapped to Devlin's. *Of course!* She'd been so worried about her sister and focused on getting to her that she hadn't thought of the connection she had to Seth. They'd always find each other. He wouldn't be able to go far.

Tuning into her senses, she tested the elastic membrane, feeling it stretch. "It's weakened."

"Follow it before it vanishes."

Diving out the window, she tumbled on the grass, springing up to speed off. "Why is it fading?"

Devlin met her, stride for stride. "You've been fighting against his bind since . . ." His eyebrows dipped as he clamped his mouth shut. "He could be diluting your blood by feeding from another. Or, he could break the bond altogether by finding a new mate. The only unbreakable bond is between true mates."

"And we weren't true mates."

"Nope."

Thank God. Sadness tainted her relief. She'd loved him with everything she'd had.

What a fool.

Shiloh and Devlin wove through the streets of LA, coming to a halt in an alley off South San Pedro Street in Skid Row. Rubbish scattered on the pavement as a cat jumped in fright, hissing at them.

The membrane pulled her another few yards down the block to a six-story brick building. Roller shutters covered the windows along the width of the first floor, spray-painted in street art. The pattern was broken in the center by a set of double glass doors, sheltered under a portico. Craning her neck, Shiloh scanned the rows of window awnings, pinpointing where Seth was.

"They're in there. Third floor, back of the building."

"He'll know you're here."

"No point being quiet then."

"We don't want her hurt. And we don't wanna draw attention to ourselves."

Shiloh's shoulders bunched as her gums ached. She wanted to rip out Seth's throat. Tear it so wide that his head hung on a paper-thin hinge. Watch all the blood he'd taken from her drain away until the leech was a dried, shriveled shell. He'd awoken her darkness and she was desperate to feed it. "How do I kill a vampire?"

"With a mortal wound. But you've gotta catch him first."

Going back to the alley for some cover, she bent at the knees and pushed off the ground, aiming for the fire escape. She crouched on the metal landing, rattling

the window. Devlin pushed her aside before sending his elbow into the glass.

"I thought we weren't drawing attention to ourselves." Shiloh narrowed her eyes.

"Just get inside."

Crunching over the broken glass, she led the way through the rooms strewn with crippled office furniture and discarded equipment. Coming to a door, Devlin pushed it open.

Shiloh's lungs seized, trapping her breath. Lanie was perched on Seth's lap, her head lolling to the side and her face swollen with bruises and cuts. One of his arms strapped around her waist, while his other aimed a gun in their direction. A couple of feet to the side, a woman's body lay twitching on the floor, blood seeping from a gaping wound in her neck.

"Polo, you blood-sucking bastard," Shiloh spat, ready to lunge.

"If you come any closer, I'll kill her." Opening his jaw wide, Seth tilted his fangs towards her sister's exposed neck. "Even if you bury her, I won't feed her. She'll die."

"What do you want?" Devlin growled.

Seth's fiery gaze turned on Devlin. "You know what I want."

Devlin ground his teeth. "You can't have her."

"Neither can you." A chilling cackle burst from Seth's throat before he turned the gun in a blur, blasting a

hole in the head of his twitching victim. The silencer muted the sound, but the vibrations still shattered through Shiloh's body. Pointing the barrel between her eyes, he continued. "Pity your sister's a bitch or I would've chosen her first."

Devlin took a step closer, pulling out a cigarette and lighting it. "You didn't choose her, because she's too young. You're stalling. You know ya can't turn her."

What the hell is he doing? Idiot.

Seth switched his aim to Devlin. "Too young to bond, not too young to die."

"Ain't no way you'll kill her. You need her." Devlin peppered smoke rings at Seth's face as he moved in closer.

Lanie moaned, her head moving an inch before flopping back down. Seth reacted by cracking the butt of the gun on the side of her skull, and Devlin lunged. In one blinding move, he'd ripped Lanie from Seth's arms and shoved her towards Shiloh. She dove to catch her, eyes half on Devlin who was holding out a clawed hand. Seth's body was thrown into the wall behind him without Devlin ever making contact.

Plastered halfway up the exposed brick like a squished bug, Seth gripped the gun, aiming at Devlin, and pulled the trigger. Devlin stumbled back with a shout, grabbing at his chest where blood spilled down his shirt, as Seth dropped to the ground in a heap.

Shiloh's eyes popped, struggling to keep up with what was happening. Adjusting her sister in her arms,

she spun and tore out of the building. She needed to get Lanie to safety.

Oh, God. Oh, God. Oh, God.

Sprinting to the nearest hospital, she prayed for Devlin to be okay. Whatever he was, he wasn't human. The way he'd thrown Seth against the wall without even touching him . . . he was powerful. Formidable. Scary as hell. If anyone had the capacity to end Seth it'd be Devlin.

But she couldn't worry about him. Her priority was Lanie. And looking at her sister's disfigured face, she cursed herself for not running faster.

The tug towards Seth continued to pull at her back, slowing her pace.

The bastard was still alive.

―――――

"I knew that boy was no good." Her dad whacked the indicator so hard Shiloh thought he might rip it off.

You have no idea. She leaned her head on her palm, watching the suburban scenery whisk by as they drove home. "You never told me."

He grunted and turned into their driveway. "I don't want to leave you here on your own with him still on the loose, but I need to get some things for your mother and sister. Mom won't leave her side, and I'm tempted to handcuff you to me so you can't go anywhere either."

"Dad, I'm tired. I'll be fine. You'll only be an hour or so, anyway. I promise to be good." It wasn't a promise she was planning to keep. As soon as he left, she was going back to find Devlin.

"I'm putting the bars back on your window."

"Okay. If that makes you feel better." *Won't stop me. Or Seth. Jax. Whoever the hell he is.*

"I'd rather brick it up. Even better—we're moving to a remote island."

She almost smiled. "You can't lock me up like a prisoner. I'm not the criminal here."

Setting free a sigh, he turned off the engine and gripped the wheel. He bowed his head, his shoulders shaking as tears dripped into his lap.

Her heart sank in her chest. "Aw, Dad." After unbuckling her seatbelt, Shiloh leaned over the gear shift, wrapping her arms around his neck.

"I can't go through that again, Shi."

She rested her forehead on his shoulder, cursing the day she'd set eyes on the devil.

"Let's get you inside." Her dad lifted his head, swiping his tears on his shirt.

"Okay."

After she gave her dad another hug and assured him for the fiftieth time that she'd be okay, he finally left. Her thoughts turned to the dark vampire. Was Devlin okay?

Detective Carter had come to the hospital to get her statement, while Lanie lay in an induced coma due to swelling on the brain. Shiloh hadn't told Carter about Devlin, wanting to keep that off the record. But, not knowing if he was okay, maybe she should have. If Carter knew anything she hadn't shared it, or let it show on her poker face.

Shiloh dashed up the stairs, swinging her bedroom door wide.

Devlin. Sprawled across her bed, he was playing with one of her trophies. He looked one hundred percent intact, although she'd witnessed the bullet hitting him in the shoulder. If he'd fed, he was probably already healed. Who knew what he was hiding under his clothes and inside his skull? She didn't want to know.

Liar.

The potent smell of his blood permeated the air and awoke her hunger, but she fought against it. She'd be damned if she let the beast inside rule over her will. That only led to misery and vulnerability at the hands of predators far more dangerous than her. Devlin had been hurt, blood staining his shirt. That was the only reason the lure was stronger, more intoxicating.

Delicious.

She cleared her throat and jammed her hands on her hips. "Are you okay?"

"Yeah." His eyes flickered with red spots, a clear sign he was lying, but if that was how he wanted to play it, she was willing to move on. She had a million questions that needed answers.

"Good. Then start talking."

Chapter

Two

Running on Empty

"What do ya wanna know?" He rubbed a thumb along the nameplate on the trophy, staring at it like if he kept rubbing, a genie would pop out and grant all his wishes.

The trophy wasn't a magic lamp; it was a relic of a life extinguished. If he wanted his wishes granted, he'd come to the wrong girl.

"I want to know everything!" Shiloh threw her arms up, wanting to strangle him. "I have no idea what the hell is going on. The only thing I do know is that Seth's not dead. I can still feel him, but only just. Where is he?"

"Gone."

"Gone? Gone where?"

"Your guess'd be better than mine." His fire-lit eyes perused her for a second before he fixed them back on the shiny object in his hands.

"What happened after I left?"

"He threatened me. I threatened him. Yada, yada, yada. He took off. I came here." The sheen of sweat on Devlin's forehead collected in beads.

Okay, so he wasn't going to tell her. But why hadn't he gone after Seth? "Why did you come here?"

"Not a clue." The trophy fell from his fingers. Red eyes flicked to hers before he shut them, leaning his head back on the pillow and clasping his hands over his chest. She watched his ribcage move in shallow bursts. If he'd come straight here after getting shot, he hadn't had a feed. His eyes told the truth in their rising crimson tide.

She lurched forward, yanking his hands apart, and pulling open his jacket. His grunt held no power. He'd folded a hand towel and tucked it over his shoulder. Red pools of blood soaked the snow-white fabric beyond redemption.

Springing to her feet, she ran into the bathroom to grab another towel, calling over her shoulder, "Shit! You're not okay. You haven't fed. You should've healed by now."

Dragging the trash can over, she dumped the soaked cloth, replacing it with the clean one. "Here, take my vein." Placing a forearm on the temporary bandage,

she leaned as much of her weight on the towel as she could before she offered her other wrist.

He opened his eyes, two depthless black holes capable of consuming her. His jaw levered open, fangs extending in sharp precision, apparently eager to strike. Her hips pulled away, the flight reflex charging through her nervous system, but her arms held firm. He needed this. She stood by her offer, even as she trembled in fear of the beast that had awoken beneath her.

"I c-can't." His eyelids slammed shut as his nostrils flared.

"What do you mean?" She pushed her wrist closer, ready to slit it herself and pour life back into him if she had to.

"You're bonded to *him*. I can't take your blood. It's contaminated. It will kill me."

Fuck. Contaminated. As if Seth had injected her with something to ward off anyone else. That was what he'd meant at the club.

She took her wrist away from his mouth and pushed with both hands on his shoulder while her brain scrambled for a solution. The possibility of watching him die was far more terrifying than becoming his prey. She pushed even harder, arms aching and brow furrowed as she prayed for help.

Carter.

The detective had given her card to Seth. *Shit, shit, shit.*

"Do you have Detective Carter's phone number?" she barked.

"Sienna. Yeah." His words faded out on shortened breaths.

He opened his eyes again. The only clue that he'd focused on her was a slight tilt of his head. There was no telling what was happening behind those ocular voids. She recoiled, instantly ashamed of her hypocrisy. He only reflected her true nature: stripped of all humanity. She and he were one and the same.

"Where's your cell?"

In answer, he tried to roll his hips, but flopped back like he was unable to hold up his weight. His chest jerked with a sodden cough. She needed to hurry. She wasn't a doctor, but any fool could see he was in bad shape. Slipping the phone out of his pocket, she grabbed his thumb, using his fingerprint to unlock the device. She scrolled through the contacts while pushing on the towel until she found Sienna, and hit the call button.

"If this is a booty call, I'm working, Dev."

"Uh, Detective Carter? This is Shiloh Howard."

"Shiloh? Where's Devlin?" Carter's voice went from hushed to all-business.

"He's been shot. He's bleeding." Blood pooled between her fingers and ran into the dips between her knuckles. He grunted as she pressed harder. *You can't die.* "A lot. Can you hurry? We're at my house."

"And you can't feed him because you're mated. Shit. I'll be . . ." The sound of rushing air drowned the urban din in the background. ". . . I'm here. Let me in."

Shiloh tossed the cell on the nightstand and bypassed the stairs with one leap, then yanked the front door open. Carter blew past her in a blur and disappeared into Shiloh's bedroom. She'd either guessed Devlin was in there, or the detective had followed her nose.

Kicking the door shut, Shiloh bolted after the cop, pausing in the doorway. Carter's dark head was bent over Devlin as she pressed her wrist to his mouth. He responded to the nourishment with groans and coughs. Each sound chipped away at Shiloh's nerves, leaving them tattered. She had to do something. If she couldn't feed him, she could at least help stop the bleeding. Armed with another towel from her bathroom, she moved around Sienna, getting in close to his shoulder. Dumping another soaked towel in the trash, she covered his gunshot wound, pressing down hard. Her face, mere inches from his, afforded her a magnified view of his fangs sunk deep into the detective's wrist. *Oh, God.* Jealousy stabbed Shiloh as deep as his bite.

Where the hell did that come from?

She looked away, her eyes moving sideways to find his scarlet stare locked on her, Sienna's gift, staining his irises. Heavy lids dropped low over his devouring gaze. He pinned her to the spot, not taking his eyes off her, even as she squirmed. She couldn't help it. Every nerve ending tingled in an erotic symphony under her skin. And he was the conductor. She had no way of

knowing, but simultaneously, no doubt he was imagining drinking from her.

Probably while naked.

His nostrils flared before he broke the stare and retracted his bite. Eyes closing, he arched his neck back into the pillow, and released a stuttered sigh.

She trembled with the surge of electricity frying her defenses into an unrecognizable mess. *This is so wrong.*

After lurching to her feet, she stepped back a few paces and held out her palms. Devlin's blood encased her hands in sanguine gloves, dripping red strands towards her wrists. With every inhale, his seductive scent worked its way across her taste buds. Smoked chili, chocolate and sin. Her hunger grew, burning in her throat. Saliva pooled in her mouth. Her fangs lengthened. She swallowed, shaking her head. She'd fed that morning. How was this possible? How awful was she to be thinking of tasting his blood when he was fighting for his life?

"Shiloh."

Her eyes sprang open, body stiffening. Carter stood in front of her, watching through narrowed slits.

Shiloh swallowed again, lowering her hands. "Is he okay?"

"I think he's going to be. I've called in a med team. They'll take him back to a facility and give him the care he needs."

She called the paramedics? When? Where are they taking him?

"A . . . human . . . med team?" *Wait until they get an eyeful of his fangs.*

And how fast he healed. How were they going to explain that to the humans?

"No. We have our own people. I need to go downstairs so I can let them in when they get here. Stay with D."

"Okay." Shiloh didn't hesitate.

Carter shot a glance at Shiloh's blood-slicked hands. "Maybe you should get cleaned up. When do you expect your father home?"

Shit. Dad. There was blood on the front door. On the floor. In her room . . . "I don't know. Soon, I guess."

The shockwaves of all the trauma had her limbs vibrating like a hummingbird's wings. Seth, Lanie, Devlin . . . it coursed through her body, building to an apex of *'What the fuck is happening to me?'* until a haze filtered her vision.

Carter frowned. "Hey, pull yourself together." The detective led Shiloh into the bathroom, tugged her arms until her hands were in the basin, and flicked on the faucet.

Shiloh watched the water gush over her palms, a red whirlpool getting sucked down the drain. Thoughts of cramming in the plug to prevent the loss of the delicacy plagued her sanity. She trapped her tongue between her teeth as her cheeks flushed in shame.

"I'll tidy up downstairs. You look after Devlin." The detective dashed off.

Breathe, Shiloh. In through the nose, out through the mouth. In through the nose—

His smell. She'd thought nothing was better than the scent of Seth's blood.

I was wrong.

She fixated on a drop of red halfway up her forearm. *Just a little taste . . .*

"Don't."

"Aargh!" Battered by the echo of his deep voice in the tiled space, she spun around to find him buckled against the doorframe. His face screwed up as he clutched the support with one hand, the arm on his injured side hanging useless by his side.

"What are you doing!? You should be lying down." She rushed over to take him by the elbow, leading him to sit on the corner of the bath and lean against the tiled wall.

He levered forward, shrugging his good shoulder in an attempt to maneuver out of his coat. "Help me get this off."

Gripping the lapels, she peeled them back, and pulled the coat down his arms behind him. Her face landed directly in line with his throat, the hiss from his mouth slithering its way down her neck. She assumed the hiss was from pain, but as she took a big step back, his sultry stare suggested otherwise. His eyes were still tinged red from his recent indulgence. Sparks of blue

added their flame as his gaze traveled around her features.

God, it's steamy in here.

She swallowed and blindly searched for the fan switch on the wall beside her. Shiloh wiped a hand across her mouth, forgetting her hands were wet and not completely cleansed of his blood. Nostrils flaring, her jaw levered open as her fangs punched free. *Shit.*

"Don't!" he barked.

"Why?" The word came out on a whimper.

"My blood will kill you, too. I can't have yours and you can't have mine. You're bonded to him."

Seth . . . fuuuuuck! She wanted to scream.

Wait—

"So, I can't drink? . . . At all?" Shiloh brought back the memory of the woman in that building, right before Seth put a bullet in her brain. She'd been bleeding from the neck. But Devlin had said if Seth drank from another it could weaken the bond. "How come Seth can drink from anyone, but I c—"

"Okay, big guy. Time to go." Carter jogged in, followed by two people dressed in coveralls rolling a stretcher.

Shiloh growled, unable to hold it in. As soon as the sound released, she hated herself for it. He needed help and she couldn't be the one to give it. Her questions would have to wait.

"Fuck off, Sienna. I don't need a goddamn ambulance." Devlin gritted his teeth as he slumped lower against the wall.

"Shut up and get on the stretcher. There's no exit wound. You need surgery if you want that bullet out."

The bullet is still in there.

He jerked forward, sucking in air and cradling his elbow. "I don't give a fuck about no bullet," he rasped. "Why ain't you out there finding that bastard?"

Carter leaned down, putting her face in front of his. "Get on the damn stretcher. I just saved your life. I can un-save it just as easily. And then who's gonna be her hero, huh?"

His mouth tightened and his eyes narrowed, flames burning the vibrant red into charred remains. Shiloh shivered as an icy chill seemed to roll off his body.

Whose hero? What did Carter mean?

"How many ya got guarding her?" Devlin demanded.

Her? Who?

"Two each shift."

"Fucking hell, Sienna." He grimaced and adjusted his shoulder. "Double it."

"You know that hospital is full of vamps. They're all on alert."

Hospital? They must be talking about Lanie. What's going on?

Shiloh wrapped her arms around her middle, needing someone to hold on to. Her throat cramped at the woeful inadequacy of the embrace. If they were going to deliver bad news about her sister, she wasn't sure holding herself together was going to be enough.

Devlin's black eyes flared at the detective before she stumbled back a couple of steps. "Fucking. Double. It."

Why was he *ordering the cop around?*

Carter planted her feet, putting her hands on her hips. "Don't push me. I'm the one helping you, asshole. Now, are you going to get on this thing yourself, or would you like us to pick you up? Might I remind you that her father could be arriving at any minute."

"Get them out of here. It's not safe."

Jesus. Mom and Dad are in danger? They'd loved Seth.

He'd loved them . . .

It had all been an act. A glossy coat of polish on a pile of bullshit.

It was Shiloh he wanted now. Why had she thought her parents would be safe? Would he stop at nothing to get her?

"Already on it," Carter replied.

He grunted and shoved to his feet, immediately falling forward. Throwing out his good arm, he slammed his elbow on the stretcher, just catching himself before his knees smashed on the ground. His body bowed, toes

pushing off the tiles, one arm holding his weight up. The two paramedics lurched forward to help him, but didn't even get close before they slid backwards and landed on their asses.

"Don't fucking touch me."

Shiloh tentatively reached out, wrapping her arms around Devlin's waist. Maybe he'd reject her like he'd done with the others, but she couldn't stand by and watch him struggle anymore.

Stubborn ass.

She helped him to his feet, turning him so he could sit on the thin mattress. His hand landed on top of her elbow, energy pulsing through his touch. Her eyes scanned his tight features. *Is he angry? Is he going to push me away? Toss me to the floor?* Her jaw dropped when he held on, tugging her even closer. She couldn't escape. Trapped in a cloud of his heady cologne, her body didn't ever want to leave. Only a tiny part of her was ringing alarm bells. The tiny part called sanity. And it was shrinking by the second. She knew he couldn't bite her. *What is he doing?*

Devlin's gaze tracked his hand as it trailed up her arm, pausing at her shoulder. For an eternity he didn't move, apart from the deep groove carving its way between his brows. His fingers reached out to tangle in her hair, gripping it tightly. Shiloh's eyes bugged out, her heart setting off in a gallop.

She should've been petrified.

She wasn't.

Her body swayed towards him. Hearing his sharp intake of breath, she watched the muscle in his jaw tick before he let go.

One glimpse of his eyes before he shut them, had her heart tripping over itself and falling in a heap of 'I should've known better.' The crimson stain had all but disappeared; the few flashes of color fizzled out as black engulfed his irises once again.

Flat. Dark. Cold.

Whatever had caused his lapse in control, it was over.

Shiloh's gut twisted. Why did she even care? She held her breath to deny his scent. Deny any part of him entry beneath the surface.

After easing his top half down until his head hit the pillow, she lifted his feet to follow. The crazy urge to climb on with him pushed its way into her mind and her muscles. She balled her fists, her lungs burning with the need for air.

Breathing—who needed it, anyway?

Nudging Shiloh out of the way, Sienna stood over Devlin. "You never learn." She shook her head and strapped him onto his transport. "You can't do this alone."

Stony-faced, he glared at the ceiling as they wheeled him out and took all the answers to Shiloh's questions with him.

Damn it.

Would he be okay?

What was going to happen to her if she couldn't feed?

And the biggest question of all . . .

What does Seth want with me?

Chapter

Three

Plan A

Five days. Six nights.

Shiloh paced the floor of her bedroom, like she'd done every night, accompanied by a festering paranoia.

Where have they taken Devlin?

Is he all right?

Have they found Seth?

Why isn't Carter answering my calls?

Pinching her nose, she begged for a moment's relief from the searing pain arcing from her nostrils to the back of her throat. The unmistakable aroma of Devlin's blood still permeated the air. She hadn't been able to

bring herself to wash the coat he'd left behind. It was hanging in her closet, the lining crusted with blood.

Turning on her heel, she marched back the other way, freeing her grip and releasing a pained groan. Picking at the dead skin on her palms, Shiloh grimaced at the bed. After they'd taken Devlin away, she'd scrubbed the quilted fabric until her hands had blistered. But the results were only superficial. She still saw him there. Those black eyes, wild for her taste and agonized at not being able to have it.

Sleep was an impossibility. She couldn't lie on the mattress, knowing that his blood had soaked its layers. She couldn't feel herself mold into the indent of his body without struggling for air, just as he had done.

He was still there. Below the surface. The smell stoked the fire building in her stomach.

It had also been five days since she'd quenched her thirst.

The last blood to touch her throat had been Seth's. She'd rather drink bleach than have his poison anywhere near her again. Shiloh tried to swallow, producing a hacking cough instead as pain ripped down her esophagus.

Burn. It burns!

Fucking Seth.

She'd messed with the devil, his brand scorching its way from the inside out. If only she'd ignored Seth that day he'd moved in across the street. She wouldn't have been reduced to a plasma junkie. If she'd never

started anything with him, her family would be safe. Lanie wouldn't be lying in a coma.

Forbidden from visiting her sister's bedside, Shiloh spent her days praying for Lanie's recovery. But it wasn't going to bring her back. For Shiloh, her state of inertia was akin to being in that hospital herself.

I can't do this.

Reaching the bed, she spun around again and headed for the window. Peering through the curtains, she noted the SUV parked across the street. It was there every night. The uninvited elephant. A signpost to the chaos ruling the Howards' lives. Nobody ever entered or exited the vehicle. She didn't know how many cops they had on surveillance, but she was damn sure she could outrun them.

Letting the curtain fall back in place, she went to the closet to grab a hoodie and her runners, throwing them on before beelining to the window. Sliding the glass open, she made a quick exit, dropping to the grass.

Shiloh's knees buckled as a hand landed on her shoulder from behind with the force of a Taser. "Where are you going?" The voice was female. Harsh. Unfamiliar.

Shiloh caged the scream before it shot from her lungs. *Shit.* She didn't turn to see who it was, eyes scanning for the best escape route instead. Her mouth dried out as adrenaline shot into her veins. Was this woman a cop? Or was she working for Seth and had somehow slipped under the notice of the watch?

Lashing out at her assailant, Shiloh landed a sharp elbow into the woman's gut. She folded forward with a grunt, her head brushing against Shiloh's hip, but didn't release her hold. Shiloh reached with her opposite arm, digging her nails into the offending hand until she hit bone. *Ugh.* Retracting her hand, she shivered, bile rising to the back of her throat.

Sorry. I'm sorry.

The woman spat a catalogue of profanities, relinquishing her grip. Shiloh launched into the air, landing with a thud on the roof of the SUV, the metal caving in beneath her. *Shit. This was not where I was aiming.* The car rocked underneath her as three of the doors opened. Four sets of red-tinged eyes glared in her direction—the woman who'd grabbed her rejoining their team. None of them were whom she needed to talk to.

Ah, crap.

Shiloh bolted. Her feet barely touched the asphalt as she sped away, two vampires on her tail. The woman—looking like a goth disciple with her black lips and heavily lined eyes—and a guy three times her size. Both of them were just as fast, just as strong, and just as determined as Shiloh. She led them in a powerful display of extreme parkour, testing her new abilities to their limits: across rooftops and down alleyways, up sheer brick walls and swinging from balconies. Her body screamed in pain, joints and muscles wrenched beyond their capabilities. Shiloh's steel will pushed her on until she made it to her destination.

Fluid Prey.

It was the only place she could think of where she might find Carter and get some answers. She slipped past the bouncers, disappearing into the writhing crowd and thumping music. Pausing to catch her breath, dancers bumped into her as she swiveled her head looking for her pursuers. Mountain man should've stood out, but she couldn't spot him. Shiloh cried for space to breathe. The room was crammed so tightly, all the faces blended into an anonymous soup. She remembered the first time she'd been there with Lanie. The night she'd realized Devlin was a vampire. The crowd had split apart, bodies piling on top of each other at the will of an unknown force. She knew who that force had been now. *Devlin.*

Ducking down, she pushed her way to the back and aimed for the booths where she'd seen Detective Carter before. Shiloh stuck to the shadows on the edges of the room. She surveyed the patrons milling around the seats, drinks in hand, bathed in the neon glow from the recessed lights above. No sign of Carter.

"Shiloh." She sucked in a breath, spinning around to find the detective frowning, hands on hips.

Carter was dressed in her pantsuit, the butt of her gun poking out from her open jacket. Not exactly a party dress. *They must've called her.*

"I'm impressed. You gave four vampires the slip. Trained police officers. I guess I underestimated you. And now you've left your parents with half the protection."

Oh, shit. I didn't think about that. "I'm sorry. Are they going to be okay?"

"We can't talk here." Carter gestured to the bar. "Follow me."

The detective took her behind the action and lights, into the dull, gray, guts of the building. The staff went about their business, ignoring the intruders as if it was no biggie to see an armed detective and a teenager in a hoodie storming through the restricted area. Passing storerooms and an office, they exited through the back entrance to where Carter's car was waiting under the cover of darkness.

"Get in." The detective opened the rear door and Shiloh slid along the leather, surprised that Carter followed her. *Why isn't she getting in the driver's seat?*

The cop slammed the door shut, cutting out the noise of the street, and Shiloh realized they weren't alone. The big guy sat in the front, firing up the engine as his feral gaze ricocheted off the rearview mirror. Beside him, the goth turned and pointed a gun at Shiloh.

She grabbed for the door handle, her gut hollowing out as she yanked with no success.

Fuck. She was trapped.

Sweat broke out on her skin and she plastered herself to the seat, the instinct to get as far away as she could a futile response.

"Put the gun away, Evren," Carter snapped.

"She fucking clawed my hand."

"She's desperate."

Desperate? She was petrified and frustrated. Why wouldn't anyone tell her anything?

"You don't know how it is," Carter added.

"Thank fuck." Evren waved the gun at the detective. "And neither do you."

What? Being kept in the dark? Having a gun pointed at your head? Being a prisoner in your own home?

Carter's mouth tightened. "Put it away." She pushed the gun aside and patted a hand on the driver's massive shoulder. "Take us to the hills."

Shiloh went taut, punching both fists into the seat. "No, you're not taking me home. Where is Devlin?"

"He was discharged a couple of days ago. He hasn't been home." Carter plucked a piece of fluff from her pants and turned her attention to the view through the windshield. "No one knows where he is."

He's gone? Fuck.

Shiloh slumped against the door, all the fight evaporating from her body.

Streaks of light scanned across her as they passed by neon lit shops on their way back to Beverly Hills. She wished the beams were capable of erasing the past. For the first time in days, she wanted to curl up and sleep. To close her eyes and go to a place where all of this shit didn't exist.

She hadn't even realized she'd latched onto Devlin as a lifeline. He'd watched over her in school.

He'd been there at the quarry, helping her uncover the truth. He'd fought for her and her sister in that old office building. He'd nearly died for her.

Now he's taken off?

What if Devlin hasn't gone? What if he was taken by Seth?

She had to stop calling him that.

His name is Jax.

They passed the turnoff to her place. She frowned, pulling her body up. "Where are we going?"

"We're not taking you home. You'll be staying with me. Our team are speaking with your parents now. We think it's best for their safety, and yours, if you're in a more secure environment. Jax is after you, not them. But he might use them to get to you. Don't worry. They're protected."

"They'll never agree to this."

"They don't have a choice. And besides, we have ways to make them agree."

"Are you threatening them?" Shiloh's voice squeaked in alarm.

"No. But vampires can be very influential when we want something. That's how we ensure our food source when we're Seekers—vampires still seeking their mate. Sometimes we need to partake in human blood if we can't find an unmated vampire. We charm our victims into wanting us to bite them. That's how Jax caught you in his spell."

Yes. He'd been a drug. An addiction. Through all those years of training, she'd honed her body and mind to be the epitome of discipline. A precision instrument able to cut through the competition as easily as she did the water. At the height of her success, Jax had proven that she couldn't completely shed her human vulnerabilities. Everybody had a weakness.

Could she learn how to control people's minds?

She clasped her hands in her lap and bit her lip, thinking of Devlin's captivating stare as he'd fed from Sienna. Was that what he'd been doing? Mind control?

The detective interrupted her thoughts. "Don't worry. It doesn't work on vampires unless the person manipulating you is your sire and your blood source."

So Devlin's seductive powers weren't some mind trick. She had no excuse for her behavior.

With a click, Evren pulled back the slide on her handgun. "Pity."

Shiloh felt the blood drain from her face, spotting the hulk's smart-ass grin in the rearview mirror.

Who the hell are these people? She squirmed in her seat. "How is that supposed to be comforting? You've just told me Se—Jax still has the ability to mess with my mind. And why the sudden change? It's been five days. What's happened to warrant the need for more security?"

The detective shifted her eyes to the view of the LA skyline twinkling in the distance. "You. You're getting weaker." Carter spoke quietly, turning her sharp

gaze back to Shiloh. "We can't risk you running after him in bloodlust. And your deterioration will soon be noticeable. We can't have your parents worrying or asking questions. We need to keep you safe until we can detain the perp."

I just need a feed.

Wasn't gonna happen.

Fuck.

She sat forward, too edgy to relax back on the seat. Besides, she had to pay attention to where they were headed in case she needed to escape.

After weaving through the streets of Los Angeles, they ended up on Mulholland Drive. From there, she lost track, breaking out in a sweat. The car took a convoluted route until they turned into a long, isolated driveway. Their progress was finally thwarted by two black steel gates imprinted with a basket weave pattern.

Faced with the imposing barrier, Shiloh reached for the door handle again—a last-ditch plea for freedom. It didn't budge. The detective raised a dark brow.

Their driver put his face up to a small screen and spoke into the intercom. The big steel gates opened. After creeping around a bend, they drove up a gentle incline past manicured gardens. Soft lights guided their way. Pale gray rendered walls came into view, segmented by large tinted windows trimmed in charcoal, and a matching roof. A stacked stone feature wall greeted them at the entry, lit by matt-black steel sconces, and embraced by lush greenery in the adjacent garden bed.

Whoa. The place was a palace. A sprawling, three-story contemporary . . . prison.

"The LAPD pays way better than I imagined," Shiloh mumbled.

Carter spoke over the duo of snorts coming from the front seats. "Sadly, no. But I do all right. I know how to invest wisely. I've been around a long time."

"How long?"

"One hundred and eighty years."

What?

Her three captors exited the vehicle, leaving Shiloh stewing on Sienna's answer.

She scrambled after them towards the house. "How long do vampires live, on average?"

"I don't know any that've died from old age, yet. Foul play, or terrible accidents are the predominant ways to go," Carter replied.

The detective opened the door and Shiloh stopped to stare as the others bumped past her and disappeared. The foyer, complete with a waterfall trickling over stone, opened into a grand room. Leather sofas held plush cushions and rested on rugs in shades of rose, pink and gray. Walls of shelves cradled rows of books. Vases and trinkets were placed sparingly. It was all beautiful and welcoming.

Still a prison.

With a tap on a touch-screen, a television lowered from the ceiling. Carter handed her the control. "Here.

Choose a channel. I'm sure you're hungry. I'll get us all something to eat before I show you to your room."

Shiloh frowned at the device, the display looked about as decipherable as her math homework. Stupidly, tears welled in her eyes and she scrubbed them away with her sleeve. No, she didn't want to watch TV. And there was no food in existence that could satisfy the hunger that eroded her gut.

Shiloh placed the control on the coffee table and followed the detective into a massive kitchen. Four refrigerators lined one wall. One of them was dedicated to wine, its glass door proudly displaying its collection. Stainless steel and cream-colored stone contrasted with deep brown cupboards in design mastery.

"Why are you doing this? Having me in your home? Why not some other safe house?"

Sienna caressed the stone benchtop, adoration in her smile. "Because I like luxury, darling."

Obviously.

The big vampire backed out of a fridge, dumping his final offering onto the banquet he'd collated, before taking a seat on a stool.

"Leave some for the rest of us." Carter chastised.

He gave her a dark look from under his eyebrows as he shoved a raw lamb shank in his mouth, shoulders hunched.

The detective grabbed a plate from the cupboard and slid it under his nose. "Shiloh, meet Lock, the

muscle of the unit. He's also pretty handy with weaponry."

And intimidating AF. "Hello."

Apparently engrossed in feeding his face, he didn't acknowledge her, or the plate.

Shiloh crossed her arms and looked around the space, wondering where the other sunshine twin had gone. Spotting a silhouette beyond the windows on a large deck, she had her answer. Against the backdrop of distant city lights, the goth had one hand up to her ear—presumably on her cellphone—and the other held a glowing cigarette.

"That's Evren. She's our sniper and Lock's mate."

They're perfect for each other.

"Do you feel like some scrambled eggs?" Carter took a carton of eggs from the fridge and placed it beside the range.

"How long will I have to stay here?"

The detective turned, her shrewd gaze holding Shiloh in its grasp. "Until we eliminate the threat." She picked up a spatula. "Eggs?"

"No. Thank you. Am I allowed to visit Lanie?"

Carter pulled a frypan out of a drawer. "No. It's too risky. I have no doubt Jax is watching your every move. Either personally, or he has people helping him." She flicked on the gas and cracked four eggs into the pan.

"Then he's going to know that I'm here. Isn't that a risk to you and your team? No offense, but a big gate and a lock on the door aren't going to stop him from getting what he wants."

God, she hoped she was wrong.

"We have cameras surrounding the premises, and sensors in the grounds, on all the windows, doors, and the roof. The entry points are reinforced and have retinal scanning technology and CCTV monitoring. The locks are manipulated remotely from our control room by one of the team. So if I come to the door under duress, the guard will not unlock it regardless of the retinal scan. The perimeter walls and gates are electrified. Yes, he can jump the boundary. But any humans he has working for him won't be able to." She sprinkled some paprika into the fluffy yellow mix. "And remember, he has to have sired a vampire, and continue to feed them, in order to control them. He can only give so much blood before he makes himself too weak. He wouldn't be able to feed more than one or two vampires at a time. We also have a team of professionals—you'll meet the rest later—and a glut of weapons. No one gets in . . . *or out* . . . without us knowing."

Carter gave Shiloh a sidelong look as she turned off the heat.

No one gets out. Got it.

"Why? Why do you have all that stuff? Is there a war going on that I don't know about? Are you related to the president? What could you possibly need all the gadgets for?"

"Oh, the toys aren't mine, darling. They're Devlin's. I live here with him."

Devlin. This is Devlin's house.

A swell of energy rippled out from Shiloh's chest at the mention of his name. She had to grab the edge of the bench to steady herself. What was it about him that had her reacting so strongly?

Who the hell was he?

And, more importantly . . . where the hell had he gone?

Chapter

Four

Visitors

She realized she'd been staring at the stone countertop when the plate of eggs slid into view. Their odor clogged her nostrils, her stomach pitching in response.

"Eat. You need food first, then sleep. Ask questions later," Carter ordered.

"I don't think I can eat." Shiloh pushed the plate away, leaning her elbows on the bench and resting her forehead on her hands.

"Sit down! Don't you dare vomit."

A hard chair bit into the back of her thighs before two massive hands pushed on her shoulders, forcing her onto the seat.

"Put her head between her knees," Carter barked at Lock.

"Stop." Shiloh held up her hands. "I'm not going to vomit. There's nothing in my stomach *to* vomit. I just . . ." She forced air out of her nose, feeling the dregs of her energy evaporate. "You know what? I'm tired. I need to go to bed."

Carter's mouth pinched. "Can you at least take an apple?"

Shiloh gave her a withering stare.

"All right. I'll take you up." Carter waved a hand for Shiloh to follow her. "Are you okay to walk?"

"Yeah, I'll manage."

Carter dipped her chin and led the way. "There are two staircases—one at the front of the house, one at the back. Your bedroom is at the rear, so I'll show you through as we go."

They passed another living room, this one more formal. It was decked out with teal and chocolate accents. Richly carved wood and sumptuous leather formed the bones of the room's style. Chandeliers dripped from the ceiling, while elaborate floral arrangements decorated the two occasional tables.

"Most of the living spaces are on the first floor. You'll find a billiards room across the hall with a bar. Access to the east wing with the gymnasium and pool are through there. We have a tennis court, but it's outside, so that's a no-go zone for you." She pointed to the next set of paneled wood doors. "Theater room."

Shiloh had to pick up her feet to keep pace with the detective as she marched along.

"Further down, you'll find offices and utility rooms. There's a basic medical facility. Myles is our medic. You'll meet him tomorrow"—she checked her watch—"later today, rather. Here are the stairs."

After ascending to the second floor, Shiloh saw a long corridor that ran the length of the house. Doors lined either side, broken here and there by a sitting room, or a powder room. Across from the landing, there was a short offshoot leading to the upper level of the east wing. A set of double doors sat at the end.

"Your room is here." Carter gestured to the first door to the right of the landing. "Devlin is in the east wing. The rest of us are that way." Carter indicated towards the front.

"Do all of you live here?"

"Not all of us. The rest of the team only stay when they're on shift. The support staff are here permanently."

"You're not in the east wing with him?"

"Oh, God no, honey. The man is a lone wolf. Nobody gets invited in there. Not even the cleaners. It must be vile. I don't want to know."

"Why don't you have a place of your own?" Shiloh bit her tongue for leaking her curiosity. "Sorry. That was rude of me to ask."

"It's a reasonable question." Carter shrugged. "We've been together a long time. We work well, so I stick around, sometimes despite my better judgement."

They've been together a long time. As lovers?

So why had he watched Shiloh with lustful eyes while he'd been drinking from Carter?

Or maybe Shiloh had been the voyeur intruding on the couple's passionate exchange. *Ugh.* She rubbed a hand over her stomach, thankful she hadn't eaten those eggs.

"Get some sleep. We'll talk in the morning." Sienna opened the door and left Shiloh to stare in amazement at her room.

Holy cow. Her bedroom at home had all the comforts a girl could wish for. This room made a mockery of her idea of luxury. There was probably a display cabinet for the occupant to store their tiara.

She tucked her hair behind her ear and stepped into the grandeur. The bed had its own floating ceiling, complete with sheer curtains. In the corner, a sitting area provided a perfect reading nook overlooking the gardens. She found a touch-screen control on an ottoman and pressed a few buttons on the menu. With a click, a discreet inbuilt cabinet across from the bed opened up. Concealed within, she had her own entertainment system. She clicked the button again to shut it.

Moving to the bed, she noticed the wall behind it didn't span the entire width of the room, leaving openings at each end. Entering on the left, she walked into a closet. The spacious room looked like a boutique

with rows of shelving for displaying handbags and shoes, yards of hanging space, and a floor-to-ceiling mirror at one end. Tucked into the shelves, a dresser mirror framed in light guarded a makeup station with a mauve bergère tucked under the bench. She walked over and took a seat to test it out. *Comfy.* In the mirror, she glimpsed a private bathroom through another door behind her.

She wandered in and spun around. The shower had its own Bluetooth connectivity with massage and steam capabilities. *Oh, yes please.* She rolled her shoulders, almost feeling the water pummeling her sore muscles.

Shiloh paused, gritting her teeth. *What am I doing?*

None of this was hers. She wasn't supposed to get comfortable here. She was being held against her will. No massage shower or state-of-the-art entertainment system could make up for the fact that she couldn't go and see her family. Her sister.

She trudged through the bathroom door, coming out on the other side of the bed. Yeah, she'd have loved to have fallen into the soft comfort it offered, but she couldn't allow herself the surrender. Not while her sister was still in a coma. Not while Devlin was missing. And not while Jax was still free to wreak havoc on everyone she'd ever loved.

Closing her eyes, Shiloh reached out with her senses, testing the pull toward Seth. It was faint, buried under piles of hatred and possibly miles of distance. Who knew the real reason for their bond's demise?

She slumped in a chair in the sitting area and fixed her eyes out the window. All she could see was a sparse scattering of stars—only those strong enough to outshine the halo of light pollution from the city. She knew she had to be as strong as the brightest star if she was going to smother Jax's plans.

Whatever they were.

She needed a plan of her own.

Rubbing her eyes, she begged for the stinging to subside. Lethargy had her in its grip. Her mind was incapable of whipping up a brainstorm while her neurons misfired under a fog of fatigue. She had no choice but to close her eyes and succumb to the exhaustion.

———

Hands deep in the pockets of his coat, Devlin stalked his way through the scattered headstones of Greyfriars Kirkyard. Under lights, Edinburgh Castle lorded over the city high on its hill in the distance. The place held too many memories, threatening his carefully constructed indifference.

Fueled with rage, each of his footfalls gouged the soft grass. He didn't give a fuck. The place was deserted. No witnesses to screw him over with their cell phone cinematography. The cool night air coiled around Devlin's vibrating form, urging him to calm down.

Not gonna happen.

The trail had led him to her.

Rubbing a hand over his aching shoulder, he swore under his breath. The fucking bullet had done a number on him. It hadn't healed right. The docs had done all they could under the circumstances.

Nobody pins me down.

It turned out painkillers didn't work on him. Go figure.

MacDonald, MacGregor, Stuart, Campbell . . . He read the names as he marched past . . . *Ross.*

There she is.

Pulling to a stop in front of a weathered sandstone grave marker, he read the epitaph.

Sorcha Ross

Beloved mother, wife and sister.

1518–1536

His body grew taut. At his feet, a patch of scorched grass held the charred remnants of a bunch of flowers. The blackened mess formed a heading for the scrawl below. Shallow channels had been carved into the earth over the grave—moats filled with blood. Their sharp angles formed an inscription of torment and warning in deep red.

The roses enjoyed the stake.

So did the witch.

You can't stop me.

Discarded a few feet beyond Sorcha's grave lay the source of the blood. An elderly man. His throat had

been torn to shreds, vessels and stringy flesh spilling out like a toppled bowl of bolognese spaghetti. The man's eyes were set in a blind stare.

Devlin's nostrils flared as he ground his teeth. Scanning his surroundings, he sniffed the air, finding nothing other than the odor of damp grass, dead flesh, and day-old blood. His vision clouded, the scene before him changing to a time when he'd called this place home.

"Devlin. Come inside. Quickly now." His mother feigned a smile as her extended arm urged him into her bosom. "We must prepare ourselves. I don't want you to worry, lad. All will be well. No matter what. I will always watch over you."

A gust of wind whipped the fall leaves around their legs as they scurried up the steps onto the porch and inside. Devlin's eyes shifted to the corner of their small cabin, finding his da watching him. The light from the hearth lit one side of his father while his other half stretched a shadow upon the wall. Both eyes glowed red, even in the dark. Something's wrong.

Mam ushered Devlin into a wooden chair, stray pieces of dark hair framing her harried face.

The door opened again. His aunt threw herself into the room and locked them in. Rubbing a palm over her swollen belly, her fretful gaze darted between them. "We must work in haste. They are almost upon us."

Devlin gripped the sides of his seat, sweat rolling down his temples despite only just coming in from the cold October air.

What was happening? Who was coming?

His father's red gaze fixed on Devlin as he shot to his feet.

"Sit." With one look, his father had Devlin's tail firmly reattached to the wooden chair. Devlin let out a whimper. It was the only thing he could do.

"Magaidh. Do what ye must." His mother held out a carving knife for his aunt, turning over her palm once it was empty.

With one swoop, the knife slashed across his mother's flesh and she let out a hiss. Aunt Magaidh locked her sister's bleeding hand in a grip over a clay bowl to collect her offering. Lines creased Magaidh's forehead as she turned to Devlin. "Give me your hand."

He tightened his trembling lips, shaking his head. She flicked her finger and his hand flew into hers against his will. "Don't be scared."

The knife cut him, ripping a cry of pain from his chest. She dropped the knife to the floor with a clatter.

After adding his blood to the mix, she bound his hand together with his mother's using rope. She held the bowl, collecting the blood dripping from their injured hands. Taking a candle, she moved the flame in slow circles under the base of the clay. Her voice rose in an incantation he didn't understand. A language he'd only heard once before when he'd snuck out to follow his mother on the night of a full moon.

His mam stared down at him, tears collecting in her eyes, her lips moving in synchronicity with his

aunt's, but making no sound. He was aware of his da rising to his feet and drawing a dagger from his coat, but Devlin's eyes couldn't stray from his mam.

The chanting stopped and his mother spoke. "*Drink.*"

Coming back to the present, Devlin spread his fingers, drawing on his power. The earth beneath his feet began to rumble. Red droplets and clumps of dirt jumped like popcorn bursting in a hot pan. Rage doused his vision in scarlet. He raised his arms higher. A potent force pumped through every cell, from the top of his head down to his fingertips, building to an untenable crescendo. Letting out a roar, he aimed the energy at the scarred gravesite. The earth exploded. A bloody mess of dirt and grass thrust into the air, landing in a shower over the graveyard. The corpse of the old man was flung back into the wrought-iron fence of a nearby grave. All traces of the desecration were replaced by a crater a few feet deep. Sorcha's headstone sat at an odd angle.

Dropping his arms, Devlin's breathing slowly returned to normal while he drew memories of her from his mind.

Her sweaty, tear-stained face as she'd greeted his entry into the world.

The sweet sound of lullabies on her lips.

Her screams of terror as she'd begged for her life.

Sorcha Ross had been his mother.

———

Shiloh woke a couple of hours later, curled in the chair at an awkward angle. There was still no sign of the sunlight over the horizon. A purple mink blanket warmed her skin, a surprise new addition. Curling her fingers into the soft fabric, she sat up, unsure whether to be thankful for the kindness or creeped out by the intrusion into her space. Her body released snaps and groans worthy of a horror film as she stretched her aching limbs.

She glanced at the bed, feeling stupid now for not answering its beckoning call, before spotting her suitcase standing near the door. Her cheeks hitched, a lightness almost lifting her out of the chair as she embraced the sight of something familiar. Something that was hers. Carter must have organized for her stuff to be brought over. *How considerate.* Shiloh's feelings towards the woman softened a little.

Dropping the blanket, she stood, shuddering as a chill washed over her. She dragged the case to the bed and plonked it on the mattress. After flipping the case open, she pulled out clothes and toiletries. She refrained from hugging them to her chest, but inside she was happy-dancing. Such a simple thing, but when so much had been taken from her it was monumental to even have her own hairbrush.

She slowly placed the items aside, distracted as her attention caught on bright-purple microfiber. *It's been a while since I've seen that swimsuit.* She draped the fabric over her hands, feeling the memories slip smoothly across her palms. She held the suit reverently, like she'd imagined holding the Olympic gold she'd been destined for. In her head, the dream had been so real it

was almost impossible to fathom that it would never come to fruition.

Who was that girl? So focused on herself and the boy she'd loved. So fixated on a picture of the future that had been sketched with a poison pen. Life had a way of toppling things that were built on shaky foundations. The pieces of her would never fit back together the same way. But that was how it was meant to be. You were meant to rise, embers bursting into flame with a renewed strength and vision. She just didn't know how the hell to do that, now that she was trapped in this place.

A soft knock sounded at the door, jerking her out of her reverie. Shiloh's head snapped around as she dropped the swimsuit back into her case. She stared at the door, rooted to the spot, half hoping her visitor would go away. The knock sounded again with more insistence.

She cleared her throat before speaking, smoothing a hand over her ponytail. "Come in."

A boy who looked to be about Shiloh's age with messy two-tone hair—brown at the roots, blond at the ends—hesitated at the entrance. Headphones tangled in his hoodie around his neck. Holding a tray in his hands, he jiggled his shoulders, and shifted the weight of a backpack.

"Err, hi. Can I come in?"

She folded her arms. "I already gave you permission."

His face screwed up and he chewed on his lip ring. "Right. Yeah, okay." He marched to the sitting area, dumping the tray on the coffee table with a clang. "Sorry.

Um, that's your breakfast. Eggs, and oatmeal, and stuff. We didn't know what you liked, so, yeah."

He looked so uncomfortable, with his eyes glued to the carpet and his hands stuffed in his pockets, Shiloh had to smile. "Thanks. Isn't it too early for breakfast?"

"Yeah, but we knew you were up. Sienna wants you to eat."

Shiloh hugged herself a little tighter, eyes widening as her breath caught. "How did you know I was awake?"

"There are sensors in each room. And, um, cameras."

They were filming her?

He coughed, his eyebrows pulling together before quickly adding, "Not in the bathroom and closet." Pink washed across his cheeks. He rocked on his heels, pivoted, and started for the door. Abruptly, he pulled to a stop and shrugged off his bag. "I nearly forgot. Here's your schoolwork. We can study together. You know, if ya want."

School? That was the last thing on her mind. "Um. Maybe."

His eyes met hers fleetingly, two tropical pools of the most vivid aqua blue. "Here." He held the pack out to her, his gaze making contact for a little longer this time. "You can keep the bag. It's new."

"Thanks." She smiled and placed it next to her case on the bed as he watched her.

He swung straight arms, then smacked a fist into his palm. "Okay. I'll catch ya later, I guess."

"Mm-hmm." She bobbed her head, watching as he walked away.

Leaving her alone.

Isn't that what you want?

She opened her mouth in a silent plea, her feet twitching to follow, but her distrust holding her steady. He was a stranger, yes. She'd been fooled before, but that was when she was still human and susceptible. Nothing about this kid set off any alarm bells.

"Are you a senior, too?" Her mouth released the words before she could twist her thoughts against doing so.

He stopped and turned, his hand half reaching for the door. "Yeah."

"Which school?"

"Beverly Hills. Go Normans." He did a half-hearted fist pump before flushing a light shade of beetroot.

She cleared her throat to stifle a giggle, deciding he was okay. But why was he here? Did he need guarding too? Or maybe he was someone's son.

"Are you under protection?"

"Huh?" His nose crinkled with his confusion. "Oh. Nope. I work here."

Her eyebrows hiked up. "Doing what?"

"IT. Nobody else really knows what they're doing. Except Ren. She's cool."

"The goth?"

His head jerked back, mouth popping open. "Ooh. If she ever hears you say that, she'll put a bullet in your brain."

"She's already threatened me with that one."

"Yeah, that's her standard welcome." He grinned and tossed his chin in the direction of the seating area. "Your breakfast is getting cold."

"Mm." She looked over. Maybe some food would be a good idea, but she didn't want him to go. The thought of being stuck here alone formed a brick in her throat. "Do you want some? I don't think I can eat the eggs."

"Yeah, I'll eat anything." He was already moving towards a chair to make himself comfortable.

She padded behind him with a soft smile on her face. "What have you been listening to?"

"Wha—?" A piece of egg flew out of his mouth with his response. He clamped his lips shut, chewing furiously before swallowing with a loud gulp. "Sorry." He reached over to grab the stray food and stuffed it back in his mouth. "Elvin Bishop."

"Who?"

His hand flew to his chest and he belted out a tune, singing about fooling around and getting bitten by the love bug.

Shiloh laughed, shaking her head. "Never heard it."

"What!? Haven't you seen *Guardians of the Galaxy*?"

"No."

His face dropped in disbelief and he pulled his phone from the pocket of his hoodie. While sliding his thumb across the screen, he disconnected the headphones. He turned the phone so she could see the album cover from the soundtrack. She read the title of the song as the melody filled her ears—*Fooled Around and Fell in Love*. Surprisingly, his rendition had been almost as good as the original.

"It's mellow. The guy sounds like a player," Shiloh commented.

"Yeah, but he's sunk now." He grinned at her.

His smile slipped as she grinned back. Dropping his gaze to the plate, he cleared his throat.

Awkward.

She shoveled a spoonful of oatmeal in her mouth for something to do. His phone chimed, lending a much-needed distraction.

Looking at the screen, he shot to his feet. "I gotta go."

"Oh. Okay then. Thanks for the food and the company."

"Yeah. That's okay." He trotted towards the door.

Shiloh pushed to her feet. "Wait. What's your name?"

"Zain with an a, i, n, as in brain. Not a, n, e, as in insane."

The corners of her mouth hitched. "Got it."

"I'll see you around, Shiloh."

The door closed with a click. She put her hand on the back of it, balking at being closed in. But this was her little bubble of safe space at the moment. She didn't really know anyone beyond that barrier. It wasn't wise to leave it open as an invitation. Not with a gun-happy gothic under the same roof.

Shiloh went back to the bed and pulled out the books Zain had delivered, their colorful covers a ruse to the dry content within. There was no way her brain would be capable of concentrating on her studies. Releasing a sigh, her eyes strayed to her swimsuit again. Could she? Would she be able to dig up her competitive spirit like she'd unearthed her body? Could she conquer her fear and find her happy place in this strange new existence?

What else am I going to do?

She headed into the adjoining bathroom and stripped off her clothes. After donning the suit, she collected a towel and robe from the hooks behind the door.

She crept through the sleeping house to the billiards room, her body tingling all the way. Everything in her bellowed, *What the fuck are you doing?* The floor

turned to quicksand as she passed the bar and gymnasium. Moving towards the entry to the pool, her sweaty palm slipped on the steel door handle. Anxiety flipped her stomach. But she wasn't stopping for anything or anyone.

The cavernous space was dark, apart from the colored lights lining the pool. Mist caressed the surface of the water and the humid air welcomed her into its warmth, loosening the knots in her shoulders. She left the lights off. Dawn would soon peer in through the glass windows.

Dropping her things on a deck chair, she toed the end of the diving board. Taking a seat, she bounced gently with her feet dipping in. Ripples circled out, overlapping each other as each gentle splash interrupted the silence. She could've relived the terror of being hunted. She could've allowed the memory to send her running for the door. But she chose not to.

Strength was always defined by the choices one made in their darkest moments. There were several options. Stand and fight. Ignore it until it went away. Surrender. Cry and moan. But it all came down to this: you either stood in your power or you gave it away to someone or something else.

She chose to stand in her power.

Fuck him.

The water called to her. It always had. She listened to its liquid song . . . and slipped in.

The warm wetness sluicing over her skin, the flex of her muscles as she pulled herself along—it was a

rebirth. She found something inside her, a fortitude beyond the physical that nobody could take away. Touching the wall, she lifted her head above the water, dragging in a breath. Shiloh slicked back her hair, a gentle smile curling her lips. She rested her head on her hands, gripping the tiled edge of the pool. She had a right to be proud after what she'd just overcome.

Hearing the shuffle of footsteps, her heartbeat doubled in time. Spinning, she watched Devlin walk towards the diving board, wearing only black swimming trunks.

Shirtless.

A purple scar bloomed where he'd been shot in the shoulder—puckered, freshly healed skin.

Thank God he's okay . . .

Her pulse refused to calm down. If he was a threat, at least she'd seen him coming this time. Her body rotated slowly, eyes following his movements. Brown skin stretched over sinewy muscle. A dusting of dark hair covered his pecs and trailed in a faint line to the edge of his shorts. His hair draped loosely around his shoulders.

She blinked.

He's way *more than okay.*

Her lips parted, tongue flitting out in search of his scent before she swallowed.

Definitely a threat.

He executed the perfect dive. His form was a shadow darting underwater for the length of the pool. He

touched the wall beside her, head breeching the surface. Her lids peeled back as his gaze landed on her. He stood to his full height with both arms raised above his head, his hands squeezing the water out of his hair. "Morning," his greeting rumbled into the vast room.

She choked in response. Face in line with his navel, she didn't know where to look, but turning away wasn't an option. Her eyes traced every inch of his body.

He's not my sire, or my blood source, but damn, he has me all twisted sideways. There was no logical explanation. It was just him. Insanely sexy Devlin. No female in her right mind would be able to look away.

"You're wet," he noted.

Oh, my God. What? Was her body's response to him so obvious? She coughed to loosen her tight throat and stood so she was a little farther away from the danger zone. "Pardon?" Now she had a close-up view of his chest. Who was she kidding? His whole body was a danger zone.

"Is this the first time you been swimming since . . .?"

Oh. Wet, as in water.

Her brow crinkled and she crossed her arms in defense against his reference. "Yeah."

"Hey, I wanted to thank you for doin' what ya did. Helping me."

"Anyone would have done the same."

He smirked. "Not true. Plenty of people want me dead."

Instantly, her hands clenched, and her fangs tingled, ready for a fight. *What the hell?* She shook off the defensive reflex and pointed to a camera on the ceiling. "Hence the need for all the security. Who are you? Why do they want you dead?"

"I ain't the best at making friends."

She snorted. *Truth.* Unfolding her arms, she leaned back against the wall and combed her fingers through the water, refraction distorting her limbs at an odd angle. "Where have you been?"

"Looking for Jax."

She tensed, pausing her movements. "On your own?"

He didn't answer. Grasping the edge of the pool beside her, he straightened out his arms and leaned his weight forward, pulling his hips back. Every muscle carved its outline into his skin.

She pursed her lips and blew out a breath, wanting to sink into the water to cool off. "Where is he?"

"I lost his trail." His eyes narrowed, glazing over for a second before refocusing on her. "Look, I know ya don't wanna be here. It'd be a hell of a lot easier on me if you weren't, but neither of us got a choice. While he's out there, you're in here. You got that?"

Her brow tightened. "Yeah, I got it." *Asshole.*

Jeez, she had crappy taste in men. *What the hell is wrong with me?* He stared down at her, eyes flicking between hers like he had more to say. By the way his jaw ticked, she'd need a crowbar to pry it out. She huffed. "So I'm just supposed to sit around and wait until you find him?"

He straightened to his full height. "You ain't sitting now, are ya?"

She sank her shoulders into the water. "Are you always an asshole?"

"Nope. Most of the time I'm a bastard."

"Agreed."

His smile split his face as he bellowed out a laugh.

She closed her eyes, letting the joyful sound sink in, somehow knowing it was a rare gift from someone so uncompromising.

"So what happens now?" she asked.

"We wait."

"What, like sitting ducks?"

"If he wants you, he's gonna have to come get you."

She forced all the air out of her lungs, leaning the back of her neck on the edge of the pool.

She was the worm on the hook.

How was Jax able to evade them so easily? They had access to the best tracking tech and the entire frickin'

police department. *She'd* been able to track him before, but now the elastic tug had faded.

I could try again.

Oh, God. Shiloh's face screwed up. She didn't want to be reminded of the burden she carried after she'd just conquered her fear of getting back in a pool. She wanted to bask in the glow a little longer before the reality of her circumstances barged in.

Who was she kidding? Reality was unavoidable. Besides, she knew this was important. Nobody wanted to catch Jax more than she did.

Reaching out with her mind, she searched for the connection she'd been sickeningly intoxicated by. She felt a pull, but it wasn't the same. It was a different consistency. More solid than elastic. The magnetic pull of two polar opposites. And it was to the man beside her. God help her, she almost drifted into him. Clearing her throat, she forced herself to block the urge. "I don't feel the bond. It's too weak."

Devlin cocked his head to the side, eyes penetrating hers. "Just try. It's still there. It ain't broken yet."

She dragged her gaze away. "I did try. Something is blocking it." *You.* "How do you know it's not broken?"

"Because you'd be dead."

Her spine went taut, water splashing around her. "What!?"

"He sired you, and he bonded you, so he can break the bond. But you wouldn't survive." He bent his

elbows and straightened them again, a fierce look in his eye. "He's not going to break the bond. He still needs you."

"For what? What is this all about?" She could barely breathe.

Devlin let go of the wall and stood up straight. "He's getting back at me."

"That doesn't make sense." She rubbed her forehead before punching the water. "You and I didn't know each other before all this happened. What have I got to do with any of it?"

"Do you remember me telling you that the only unbreakable bond is between true mates?"

"Yes."

"And that he ain't yours?"

"Get to the point, Devlin."

He ground his teeth before answering. "You were supposed to be mine. He took you from me."

She blinked, her jaw loosening.

Part of her wanted to spit profanities and tell him she had a right to choose who she wanted to be with. That she wasn't his, or anyone's to take. But the rest of her, the core of her being, knew otherwise. Her reactions to him were too strong. Too unrelenting. She couldn't stop them, even at the most inappropriate times.

He gazed back, sparks of color lighting the dark depths of his eyes where his soul bared itself. "You feel the truth, don't you?"

Shit. Without a doubt.

Her chest throbbed with the truth while her mind brought forward every reason to deny it. "But you don't even like me."

"I never wanted this." His Adam's apple jumped. Scrubbing a hand over his stubble, he looked away.

His tough façade lifted for a second, and she had a glimpse of what he'd been hiding.

He didn't want this?

Bullshit.

She saw *want* written in his eyes. In the jump of his pulse under his skin. In the way his muscles strained. The field of power surrounding him ploughed into her, tempting her to come closer. But all he did was stand before her.

Heart pounding, energy surging, her body wanted to slam into his and meld them as one. She could blame biology, but it went deeper. She didn't budge. She just stared, her brain trying to figure out the logic of what her soul already knew.

But why hadn't Devlin stepped in sooner and saved her?

Why was she really here, under his roof?

The roof he shares with his lover.

How could she trust her feelings? How could she trust him when his mouth said one thing and his body spoke of something else altogether? After the horror of Jax's betrayal, why would she even *want* to believe

Devlin? Why surrender to a fate she didn't choose when there was no possible future anyway?

Her heart hiccupped as her ribcage deflated. After easing her body down into the water, she dipped her chin into the warm liquid, giving herself a moment's pause. "So what happens now? I can't break the bond. I can't even feed."

I'm going to die, aren't I?

The unspoken question plugged her throat.

He didn't have to answer. The sparks in his irises fizzled out, fading to black.

I'm toast.

Tears pricked Shiloh's eyes as she buried an impending sob deep in her chest where it would never escape. What was the point of setting her pain free when she'd never be free herself? She'd been robbed. Her future, ripped away. Her past, sabotaged. She'd never have a chance to take fate up on its offer.

The water seemed to thicken, feeling more like slime on her skin. Her moment of bliss had been ruined. Again. Why had she even tried diving back in?

Fucking vampires.

Shiloh ducked under the surface and kicked off the wall, torpedoing to the deep end. Climbing out, she wrapped herself in the towel and sat on the chair, focused on a place in her mind where she never wanted to go again. That cold, damp hole in the ground. The soil smothering her, pressing its weight so she could barely move. She'd died before. But she only remembered the

pain of the moment of death and the horror of the moment of waking up. She couldn't remember the in-between. What if she hadn't woken up? Would she have simply ceased to exist? Or would she have found peace in some other plane of existence?

Devlin crouched at her feet, resting his hands on the chair beside her thighs. "We're gonna find him. I'll make him feed you."

"I'd rather die," she whispered.

"Don't say that." His voice cracked.

She raised her eyes to meet his pained stare. "It's the truth."

Curling his hands into fists, he cursed and hung his head. "I want to kill the motherfucker, but I can't."

Because of me. "He needs to die for what he did to me and Lanie. And who knows how many other lives he's ruined. He *will* die. I don't care if that means the end of me too. I'll do it myself."

"He ain't gonna get close enough for you to do it."

"Do you really think you can stop him with some sensors and a few extra guards? I got past four of your guards and made it all the way into town. What's to stop him from jumping the fence, taking out the cameras and the guards, smashing a window, and grabbing me? He'll be gone in a second."

"Bullet-proof windows."

Her mouth twisted. He had an answer for everything. Except they weren't the answers she wanted.

"You can't keep me here forever. And how much time do I have anyway? If I die, he won't be coming after me anymore, and you can kill him."

"If you die, he'll go after Lanie."

The room warped as the blood drained from her head. She pulled her legs up onto the chair and rotated on her butt to free herself from the cage of his arms. She had trouble moving her dry tongue to speak. "What does he want with us?"

Devlin dropped his arms onto his thighs, glaring at his clenched fists. "He wants to bring me down. It ain't about you or your sister."

So I have to die because of some spat between two boys?

Anger simmered under her skin, itching her all over. She bored holes in the top of his head, wanting to drill through his armor and into the truth. He didn't look up. Or wouldn't. Was he wracked with guilt? Or was he lying?

Either way, she'd had enough of the conversation.

She lowered her feet off the side of the chair, grabbing her robe. "I can't—" Chewing on her lips, she took in a sharp breath through her nose and sped off through the house to her room.

Wrapping herself in the robe, Shiloh collapsed on the bed and shut her eyes. Her weight sank into the mattress as his revelation shredded her heart.

I'm going to die.

And if she couldn't kill Jax first, Lanie was in danger. All because Shiloh had been earmarked as Devlin's, and Jax was on some sick revenge bender.

There were no words.

Not even the four-letter variety were adequate.

She lay there letting it all eat away at her, thoughts pinging around her brain with only one solution popping up time after time. She had to kill him before she died.

Her head throbbed with the buildup of pressure. She dug her thumbs into the hollow under her eyebrows in a bid for relief, but that only made it worse. She was famished, exhausted, pissed off, and apparently, staring death in the face. What the fuck was she supposed to do? How could she get out of here and get to Jax before he got to her, or Lanie?

She couldn't give in. But if she didn't calm the hell down, the grim reaper would be dropping by way earlier than required.

Calling on years of training, she used breathing and relaxation techniques to reduce the tension in her body, and quiet her galloping mind. Every time a thought materialized, she brushed it away, denying the worry and the fear until she wasn't sure she existed anymore.

That would be true soon enough.

Suddenly, her body slid a half an inch towards the window. Her eyes sprang open, roving the room for an intruder, arms lifted in defense. She was alone. She got up and checked the hallway. *No one.* After moving over to the window, she scanned the yard. The yard was bathed in fall's early morning sunshine. From the corner of her eye, she thought she saw something near the boundary wall. Her gaze tracked a crow as it left its perch in a nearby tree and glided down to pick through the grass.

Just a bird. I'm going mental.

She tried to turn away, but her body toppled forward into the glass. "Oomph!" *Ouch.* Her body turned ice cold. She knew that feeling. It was the elastic membrane urging her in Jax's direction. Cheek squished to the window, she peered out of the corner of her eye, catching a flash of golden blond just above the wall before it vanished over the other side.

Fuck. It's him.

Jax had found her.

Body quivering, she managed to peel herself off the glass. With bulging eyes, Shiloh scanned the boundary line, waiting to see the silver of the reaper's sickle as it caught the rising sun.

He still had power over her.

The bond may have weakened, but so had she.

She had less time than she'd thought.

Chapter

Five

Team Player

Surging with adrenaline, she sped downstairs and into the kitchen before rearing to a halt. Two strangers turned to stare at her. A short guy with tight brown curls and a bushy beard sat at the bench with a cell in hand. Standing at the glass wall overlooking the side yard, a tall, blonde warrior princess cradled a steaming mug.

The guy placed his phone on the bench and came over. "Good morning."

Shiloh ignored him and ran to the walk-in pantry, finding it empty. "Where's Devlin? Or Carter?" Her blood hammered on the walls of her veins. *Where are they?*

She didn't wait for his answer, dashing through to the adjoining formal dining before coming back in when she didn't find either of them.

"Carter is at the station. Devlin has gone. I'm Myles."

She pressed her fists into her temples. "Gone where? Jax was here. We have to go after him."

"Yeah, we know. We saw him coming. D's on the hunt. He won't get far," the blonde interjected.

"What!? Is anyone with Devlin? What if he gets hurt again?" *Oh, God.* Shiloh sucked in shallow puffs of air, unable to get enough.

"Honey, calm yourself." The warrior princess came over and slid a muscled arm over Shiloh's shoulder, blocking her path. "You need to stay here where we can protect you. If you run out, fangs blazing, it's no help to D at all. First thing you need to do is get dressed. I know you're fond of walking around in your one-piece, but let's leave something to the imagination." The woman gently pushed at her back, but Shiloh resisted, eyes dropping to see that her robe was open.

She rectified the wardrobe malfunction before shaking off the blonde's embrace. Taking a defensive step backwards, she crossed her arms.

"Give her a break, Margo," Myles protested.

Frustration beat a relentless rhythm inside Shiloh's head. She pinched the bridge of her nose. "How do we know what's happening? Who's with him?"

"Ren is with Zain, tracking them in the control room. Carter is using all the resources at her disposal to help us out. Devlin has Lock with him," Myles answered.

"Where's the control room?"

He tossed his curly head. "I'll show you. I was on my way there anyway."

Shiloh followed Myles past the billiards room and into the theatre room at the back of the house. Heavy, pale gray curtains lined the room, filled with three rows of recliners all facing a massive screen. He walked down the aisle to the right and pulled a curtain aside to reveal a door. Putting his face up close to a scanner on the wall, he released the lock and let her in. It led down a set of stairs and through another door.

Cold air immediately seeped beneath her skin, coaxing her hairs on end. Pulling the edges of her robe together, she looked around. Set in a grid pattern above a desk, several monitors lit the room. Tall racks of computer servers stood to one side with colorful wires bound neatly in twisted coiffures that trailed down their backs. Tiny lights flickered as the technology did its thing.

Evren sat in front of the screens wearing a headset like a receptionist, talking into the microphone. "He's heading east on Wiltshire Boulevard." She tapped on a keyboard and the images on some of the screens changed. Shiloh recognized MacArthur Park Lake, and on another display, the Los Angeles Public Library. But most of the monitors showed different rooms in the house.

Zain occupied the chair next to Evren. He shot a look at Shiloh. His eyebrows climbed, eyes detouring to Evren, before he went back to driving his mouse.

"What's she doing in here, Myles?" Evren snapped without diverting her attention.

"She saw Jax. She knows what's going on."

Evren huffed. "No, she doesn't. She has no idea."

Shiloh curled her fingers into a fist, wanting to claw the goth vampire's face so that it matched her hand. If someone didn't tell Shiloh the truth sometime soon, she was going to lose her shit. She turned suspicious eyes on Myles, figuring he was the easiest target.

He cleared his throat and scratched behind his ear, not looking away from the screens. "Zain is our tech whiz kid. He's the reason we have access to the city's network of CCTV cameras, so we can see where they're headed."

Shiloh stared hard at the video. "I don't see them anywhere. How do you know where they are?"

"Ren knows what she's looking for. To the human eye, it might look like a glitch on the screen." Myles shrugged. "You've gotta be quick. Plus, we're using an app to track Devlin's cell. Jax is smart enough to have gone off-grid. He's probably using a burner phone. He has to have a way of contacting his team. He can't be working alone."

Evren muttered into her microphone and jabbed at the keys on her keyboard before the image of the lake changed to City Hall. "He stopped. Why did he stop?"

she mumbled to herself, eyeballing the video feed before pushing the headphone closer to her ear. "D. Yep?" She frowned and brought up a map of LA on another screen. "Grand Park Station is near there. He could have gone underground." Again, her fingers flew over the keys and another two screens changed to show commuters packed into carriages on their early morning travels. "Yep, getting a visual now." Two more screens showed the platforms lined with people waiting for their train.

Shiloh leaned forward, gripping the edge of the desk. Zeroing in on each of the nameless faces, she saw people engrossed in their phones, chewing their nails, holding novels. Every hint of blond had her narrowing her eyes, but none of them had Jax's familiar features.

"Running facial recognition." Zain worked some magic on another keyboard and brought up a picture of Jax. He grinned at her from the corner of the screen, a snapshot of his time as a student, while the rest of the screen scanned the footage of the passengers.

Shiloh reared back, an unstoppable reflex reaction. She was standing here hoping to find him among the crowd, but when confronted with the face of the boy as she'd known him, she felt the sting of betrayal all over again.

Shiloh's left foot slid backwards, but not by her choice. Her stomach dropped. She dragged her leg forward, fighting against the pull. This time, her right foot slid back. She swallowed, turning to the door. *It's the bond.* "He's not there."

"We don't know that yet. Give it some time," Evren growled.

"No, he's not there. I can feel him close."

Shiloh opened the door, racing out of the theatre room just as gunshots pierced the quiet. She bolted into the billiards room next door to get a look through the windows. A cluster of bodies, guards dressed in black, and vampires who didn't belong, tangled in a fight for supremacy. Dirt showered them as figures flew through the air, gouging tracks into the grass on landing. More gunshots left two guards and one of the vampires on the ground, blood pouring from their peppered carcasses.

Margo broke away and charged at a young guy holding a gun. His eyes bugged out before she punched him directly in the throat. His head snapped back looking like it was about the detach clean off his neck before he crumbled to the ground.

"Stay inside!" Barging past a frozen Shiloh, Ren pulled a gun from behind her back and exited through an external sliding door.

The rest of the pack broke up as two intruders fled. Evren joined four guards in pursuit. She threw out her arms to signal, and yelled instructions for them to split up in different directions. One went with her and disappeared over the wall, following the escapees. The other guards spread evenly around the perimeter of the property, guns pointed to the sky.

Margo crouched over the kid she'd felled as he writhed on the ground. Shiloh's jaw dropped. *How is he still alive?* After putting him in handcuffs, the blonde went to stand before another shot rang out. Blood and flesh exploded from Margo's leg, sending her toppling to the earth. Within a second, the kid had disappeared.

Shiloh blinked. *Where did he go?* The guards came running, pumping off a few rounds over the wall, but it was too late.

She didn't see him jump. He couldn't have jumped.

What the hell just happened?

Shiloh chewed her lips, hands pressed to the glass. *Do I go outside and help? What if Jax comes back?* She felt for the tug. It had faded. If Jax *had* been there, he was gone again.

Fuck it, I'm going out.

Shiloh yanked the door open, pulling the sash from her waist, and sprinted over to Margo. Stemming the bleeding with the makeshift tourniquet, Shiloh assessed Margo for any other injuries.

"I'm okay, it's just a graze." She shooed her off.

Shiloh's eyebrows climbed as high as they could get. "It's a gaping hole! I'm going to pick you up and take you inside."

The warrior scoffed and combed her fingers through her cropped white-blonde hair. "I can walk."

Shiloh ignored her and scooped her arms under Margo's knees and back, but as she stood, she squealed, shocked to find Devlin looming over them. He took Margo off her hands and thundered across the yard. She saw the hellfire burning the black of his eyes as she ran to keep up.

Ren landed on the grass behind him, following in their wake. "We lost them."

"No shit," Devlin spat.

The goth slowed her steps and shot a foul look at Shiloh before stalking back towards the carnage.

Still several feet away, Devlin flicked a finger at the sliding door before it slammed open, apparently at his mental command. Her whole body tingled, caught in the waves of power he emanated. She remembered how he'd flung Jax against a wall without touching him. If Jax hadn't had the gun, he'd be imprisoned right now.

After carrying Margo through the billiards room, Devlin headed down the hallway to the bowels of the house. Shiloh stuck with them, hoping she could help in some way. They reached the last door, the barrier automatically swinging wide to allow Devlin to enter.

White tiles lined the empty room with benches and cupboards tucked around its periphery, and a gurney in the center. Shiloh watched from the hallway as he laid the patient down, and Myles slipped inside to attend to her. Tossing around the idea of stepping in, Shiloh teetered on her toes and gnawed on her lip. What could she do? She sure as hell couldn't give blood. She'd done her first aid course, but applying pressure to stop the bleeding was as far as her knowledge went. So why was she still standing there?

Devlin stepped away from the gurney, turning icy black eyes in Shiloh's direction. Her hair stood on end, a chill washing over her. There was her answer. She wasn't welcome. Placing her hand flat on her stomach,

she leaned back on the wall and watched as he raised his hand to slam the door. The harsh sound delivered an audible slap in the face. The solid barrier between them appeared to grow as the hallway shrank around her. He had a right to be angry. This was her fault. People were getting hurt because of her. People had *died*. It was guilt that had her rooted to the spot, sure as if she'd held the gun herself.

How many more had to die before Jax could be stopped?

She walked slowly up the stairs and back to her room, letting her thoughts run riot. She had to stop this. Somehow. She wished her sister was there to help her think it through. Lanie would've already broken out. Or at least be planning to. Shiloh had evaded them when she'd escaped from her house. But if she managed to get past all the security here, she knew Devlin would lead an army of vampires in search of her. So many more lives would be in danger.

Trudging to her bed, she went straight to her suitcase to grab some clothes before soothing her worries with a warm shower. Dressed in a loose T-shirt and running shorts, she sat on the mattress and emptied the remaining contents of her suitcase. Two pairs of tennis shoes, another swimsuit, a couple of pullovers and jeans. A scarf . . . it was only September. The cool weather didn't really start for another couple of months. How long did her mother think she'd be gone? She put all the clothes away in the closet, along with the empty case and returned to sort out the rest. Her laptop, the novel she'd been reading, and a notebook were the only things left.

Opening the notebook, she recognized Lanie's handwriting. In neatly printed capitals, the words, *WHO IS DEVLIN?* headlined the first page. Under that she'd drawn a triangle, writing names at each point—Shiloh, Seth, and Devlin. And inside the triangle . . . a question mark.

Damn, that girl is smart. Lanie had been questioning the connection before Shiloh even realized there was one. Now she knew that Jax was using her for revenge. But what did he plan to do with her? Kill her? If it was as simple as that wouldn't he have done it already? And why, if she died, would he then go after Lanie? How was that going to hurt Devlin? She wasn't his mate.

Shiloh flipped the page to find more of Lanie's writing.

Devlin Vice. No middle names.

Born April 11th, 2000. Birth certificate unobtainable.

Lives in The Flats.

Shiloh paused, looking out the window. *The Flats?* That was bullshit.

How the hell had Lanie gotten his information?

Shiloh's eyes dropped back to the page.

Transferred from Salt Lake City 4 months ago.

<u>Around the time of Shiloh's disappearance!</u>

Not on social media.

Who is he?

That last question was circled in red ink.

Shiloh let her arms fall, slapping the book on her lap, and stared ahead. *Yeah, who the hell is he? If the address is bogus, the rest probably is too.*

The look on Devlin's face as he'd shut her out replayed on Shiloh's mind. Like it was all her fault that Jax was after her. That Margo had been hurt. And Shiloh had stupidly blamed herself for it when her finger should have been pointed at his snarly face. This was all about him and Jax and some sort of rivalry. The fact was, she was innocent in all this. And so was Lanie.

Letting her anger boil, she sprang off the mattress. Nobody goes in the east wing? *Yeah, fuck that.* She was going to uncover his secrets. If no one was allowed in his room, he must be hiding something.

She had a right to know. She'd search the house until she found something. Anything to explain why the hell her life had been blown apart because of some teenage vampire's hard-on for revenge.

She glided silently across the hallway and down the short corridor to his wing. Jiggling the door handle, she found it locked. *Damn.* She didn't have the tools or the know-how to pick a lock.

She tried it again to be sure, and it opened. *Weird.* She peered through the crack of the door before slipping in, closing it behind her. She scanned the room, slack-jawed.

What?

The room was huge.

And empty.

Light streamed in from the north and south windows, making stretched rectangular patterns on the light gray carpet. She stood with the sun warming her feet, getting her bearings for a second. The east wing had to be way bigger than this one room. The level below it encompassed the billiards room, the gymnasium, and the pool. She noticed a set of frameless double doors with concealed hinges at the far end of the room.

Pushing into a bedroom, she stopped short again. The single occupant of the room—a mattress on the floor—appeared like a small boat adrift on a gray carpet ocean. She'd come here to search for clues, and it didn't look like she was going to get any. Unless there was something hidden under the bed.

The room was much smaller than the gymnasium and pool, but she guessed there was a bathroom and closet beyond the far wall, similar to her room. Walking past the mattress, she headed to the left side. In her room it would have been the entry to the closet. In the east wing it was the opposite. She found herself in the bathroom. It had dark gray walls paired with sunny yellow patterned tiles, and white benchtops. A deep spa bath sank into the floor. It looked like it could take four people, and hours to fill. He also had a steam, massage shower, but it was built for two. She found a bar of soap, a bottle of shampoo, and a towel, as the only evidence that the room was in use. Opening a drawer between the two sinks, she found a comb, a razor, and a stick of deodorant. No shaving cream. No aftershave. No moisturizer. He stuck to the basics. There were no clues

as to who he was. It was like he was a visitor in his own home.

After shutting the drawer, she clasped her hands together before she touched anything else. Maybe she'd find something in the closet, but she couldn't go in there. The anger drained out of her system, replaced by self-recrimination. *What am I doing?* She was so far out of line. She'd disrespected his privacy when he'd accommodated her and kept her safe. He had a right to be pissed off that his people had been hurt.

A male voice interrupted her snooping. "Couldn't find what ya were looking for?"

Chapter

Six

Sprung

"Shit! Devlin." She spun around to find him leaning on the doorframe between the closet and the bathroom, a sneer on his face, and flickers of red in his eyes. "I wasn't . . . Okay, yes I was. I'm sorry." She backed towards the door to the bedroom, but before she could blink, he was there, arms and legs spread, blocking her way. Waves of dissent rolled off him, pressing on her body. Instead of backing down and giving him all the power, she harnessed it, stirring a ball of fire in her gut. She frowned, watching his chest heave with each breath. "I said I'm sorry. Please move aside."

"No."

Her head jerked up and she found his intense crimson stare aimed at her mouth. Her whole body buzzed as her legs turned to jelly. She swayed, reaching for the wall to steady herself.

Moving so fast he was a blur, he clamped his arm around the back of her knees and threw her over his shoulder, dragging a scream from her lungs.

"What are you doing?" She grabbed onto the back of his shirt, her body bouncing with each of his strides.

"Puttin' you back where ya belong."

Where is that?

She ended up back across the hall, flung onto the bed in her room.

Folding his arms, he crowded the space at the end of the bed. "Why were you in my stuff?"

"I don't trust you."

"You ain't so trustworthy yourself. Your dad should've put those bars on your windows a long time ago."

Shiloh huffed, scooting back to sit up against the pillows. *How dare he?* "What, so you've been spying on me this whole time?"

"Babe, I got better things to do with my time."

Her eyes narrowed to slits as sharp as a blade. "Why should I trust you?"

"I'm a stand up guy." His face held no hint of humor and all the marks of an impending explosion. Red

eyes, bulging veins, elongated fangs. If she wasn't so angry, she would've been running for her life.

"You're not a guy."

"Not even close."

"Can you blame me for wanting to know who's holding me hostage?" She got onto her knees and threw a finger in his face. "How are you any better than Jax? Both of you want me for your own means."

"I'm tryna keep you alive and what did you do . . .?" Locking his palm around her forearm, he shoved her back onto the pillows. Shiloh landed with a grunt. "You ran straight out into the fucking fight."

"Margo needed help and I knew Jax was gone."

"How? You can't trust the bond anymore. You're too weak and he's masking it."

"I know what I felt." Her voice went quiet, all the fight draining from her.

Devlin circled the bed, planting both fists into the mattress either side of her torso. Shiloh dragged in a breath and froze. What was he going to do? She sensed conflict in him. In the way he dug into the bed beside her but didn't touch. In the stiff set of his shoulders and the turbulence in his gaze. He wanted to consume her. Was it out of anger, or hunger? Or was he looking for a way to torture himself? Both of them knew he couldn't take what he wanted. And damn if she didn't want to cry at that truth. Because for all the bliss she'd felt with Jax, it had been false, like she'd been hooked on a drug—an artificial high. But with Devlin the pull was electric, like

she was plugged into the essence of life itself. She wanted to consume him, too.

Did she trust her instinct?

Hell, no.

Could she fight it?

Nuh uh.

Her fangs lengthened in readiness. She corralled a cry of hunger in her throat. It wouldn't do either of them any good to release it. Scarlet stained her vision, just as it stained his. Trembles overtook her as tears welled in her eyes.

The sharp planes of his face seemed to soften, and his fingers flattened, scooping under her in a tender embrace. The red in his irises drained away, making room for flickers of color in that dark midnight gaze before his lips pressed gently onto hers.

Holy shit. The contact lit her body on fire. Her starvation was all but forgotten with the gratification of a different appetite. Releasing a moan, she hooked her arms around his neck.

Pressed chest to chest, their heartbeats galloped in a race nobody could win. A race they had no business starting. She sensed that he knew what she was thinking, but his lips didn't leave hers for a second. He didn't push or ask for anything more. She didn't feel crowded. She felt safe. In that moment, he exposed a side of himself she wouldn't have believed existed. He could be gentle and caring. He was protecting her, like he'd done from the start.

She pulled back to suck in a breath. "I don't even know you. Why does this feel so right?"

"'Cause it is. Instincts don't lie."

Doubt struck her heart, flushing the desire from her system. She'd believed the feelings she'd had for Jax. Her instincts hadn't been her own. How could she ever trust them again? "They do when they've been hijacked." Shiloh pushed against his shoulder. "You were angry with me."

He huffed and eased his head up so he could look at her. "You were outside. That ain't no place for you. Not while that asshole is still alive."

"I was trying to help."

"You put everyone in more danger." Lying on his side, he tucked her in close. "I was more pissed at me for fallin' for his goose chase. Won't happen again." He flicked a finger and the curtains shut.

She wondered if she could do that, too. Concentrating hard, she pointed her finger at the curtains, willing them open. Her bottom lip popped in a pout when they didn't budge.

He smirked, grabbed her finger, and sucked it into his mouth before nipping the tip. "Sleep."

After you just did that? She'd felt that nip between her legs, and squeezed her knees together to stop the sensation. "I'm not tired."

Besides, how could she sleep in a bed with him? Yeah, he had protected her and there was no denying their connection, but he was withholding something. She

couldn't trust him. This whole spat between him and Jax . . . there was more to it. And the trauma of betrayal from her ordeal was still fresh in her mind.

Her jaw levered wide as she yawned. God, she *was* exhausted. How long had it been since she'd had more than a couple of hours of sleep? Nearly a week? Her eyelids drooped. "You should leave." Already drifting off, she turned her face into his shoulder, getting more comfortable without thinking.

"Sleep," he whispered into her hair, his voice the perfect lullaby to send her off into a dreamless slumber.

———

Alone in a strange room, she awoke to silence and darkness. It took her a minute for her eyes to adjust and to get her bearings. *Devlin's house. Where is he?* The air was layered with his delicious scent. Her stomach grumbled. Damn, this was some kind of torture being so close to the candy store and not being allowed in. She touched her fingertips to her lips, remembering the tenderness in his touch. How close they'd both been to slaking their thirst. But both of them knowing it would end in death. If she was going to die, that'd be her method of choice. Death by liquid ecstasy. When it was time—when Jax was captured—she might just do it.

Shiloh sat up, her muscles cramping with the movement. When she reached upright, the room continued to tilt as the blood drained from her head. *Whoa.* She folded her legs, slapped her hands on her knees, and stuck her head down. It was day seven without a feed. How long could vampires go without a

drink? How long until she died of starvation? Pulling in air through her nostrils, she waited for the spinning to stop before heading to the bathroom. This was nothing compared to what Lanie was going through. She needed to remember that. And her poor parents must be beside themselves. She prayed that they were okay.

In the mirror, her pale face seemed foreign, and she barely registered the feel of the cool liquid wake-up call she splashed on it. Leaning over the basin, she peered at her reflection. Glazed eyes returned her stare. Maybe she should go back to bed.

"You're awake." Devlin wandered in from the bedroom.

Her stomach buzzed with a swarm of nerves. Had they actually kissed or had that been a dream? If that was what happened in her dreams she'd sleep for eternity. "Yeah." Shiloh eyed him in the mirror before snatching a towel to dry her face. And hide. He was a god who'd strayed far from heaven, but if anyone was stupid enough to go looking for a halo, they'd be sorely disappointed. She didn't want him to see her, sallow and fading under the LED lights.

Vulnerable.

What the hell was she thinking, having fantasies about being with him?

Two strong palms gripped her forearms, unveiling her from his sight. "Gonna be no skin left if you keep rubbing like that." He dumped the towel on the bench and grabbed her by the hand. "You gotta eat

somethin'." He tugged her towards the door, but she resisted.

Sleeping together . . . holding hands . . . what were they doing?

There was no future for them. There was barely a past.

She dropped his hand, but he picked it up again, rejecting the distance she'd imposed. "What's the matter?"

"I don't—" She lowered her gaze to their clasped hands and chewed her lip. "I don't think it's a good idea to get attached."

"It's too late for that and you know it. We've been attached since before we met. That's why Jax's hold on you weakened after you saw me for the first time. You recognized me. Do ya remember that day in the coffee house?"

Her brow creased. Heck yeah, she remembered. She'd been desperate to see Jax when a whirlwind of energy had sucked her in. And then she'd heard Devlin's voice, his deep grumble yanking her from her seat with force. "But I'd never seen you before."

"Nope. But it ain't important. You knew who I was to you. You know."

She pulled away again and this time he let her. "I know nothing. Is Devlin even your real name? Why do you live in this massive estate, but sleep on a mattress on the floor? Where did you come from? Who are your family? I know *nothing* about you."

"See, that's your problem. Ya gotta switch this off—" He tapped her on the temple. "—and listen to this instead." He punctuated his statement by thumping a fist on his stomach.

Had he almost cracked a smile? "My belly? It has nothing to say because it's empty."

His cheeks did a slow climb. "Then let's go fill it." He tugged her behind him and out through the bedroom.

"Are you going to answer my questions?"

"Devlin is my real name. I didn't buy this house for me. I don't give a shit if I have to sleep on the cold, hard ground. I needed somewhere secure."

She jogged every couple of steps to match his pace as she processed what he'd said. *He didn't buy the house for himself. So all the security* . . . Shiloh got goosebumps all over as a possibility came to light. He'd been planning to steal her away. Devlin knew what Jax had been doing. Had he bought the house for her so she'd be safe?

At the top of the stairs, she pulled on Devlin's hand to stop him and raised wide eyes to his questioning stare. "Who did you buy the house for?"

He didn't blink. Or move. And the longer she waited, the more his gaze honed in like a laser beam until she thought she'd burst into flames.

"You."

He came at her unexpectedly, his mouth covering hers in a bruising kiss. She grabbed onto his arms before

she hit the floor. His tongue thrust into her mouth, demanding and giving at the same time. His taste seeped into her brain, just about lifting the top of her head off. Kissing him was like skydiving for the first time. Mind blowing. Thrilling. Fucking terrifying. But there were no clear skies on this dive. No unhindered path to redemption. It was as if a tornado opened up beneath them, kicking up hemorrhaging corpses and bloodied mattresses, death sentences and psycho exes—all the reasons this was a bad idea. As much as she wanted to freefall into him, to just let go and follow her body's instincts, it had to stop.

Her jaw tingled in warning and she panicked, pushing against his chest. But she was too late. Her fangs shot out, scratching his lip.

"FUCK!" He jerked back, licking away the crimson evidence of her misdeed.

"I'm sorry! I couldn't stop them." Nor could she stop the tears from welling in her eyes. This was beyond cruel. She had the promise of nourishment in front of her and she couldn't take it. And she'd hurt Devlin.

"Babe, if you think you upset a vampire by biting him, you got a lot to learn. I ain't worried about me. But if my blood mixes with his blood in your veins, that ain't gonna end well. My guess is that it'll speed up the process."

"Oh, shit."

"Yeah. We gotta go see Myles." He headed for the stairs again. "I was a dick for kissing you like that. I'm sorry. It's fucking torture trying to control myself

around you." He stopped halfway down and pulled her into his arms.

She couldn't hold herself together anymore. Letting her tears spill, she sank into his embrace and cried.

Chapter

Seven

Answers

"How bad is it, Doc?" Shiloh pushed on the cotton ball in the crook of her elbow, watching Myles label the vials of blood he'd just taken.

"I won't know until I've received the results from the lab. Your vitals are all fine. I don't see any changes in your eyes that have me concerned. We'll just have to sit tight. In the meantime, make sure you keep eating and drinking regularly. It's a pity we can't give you any blood, but we have to work with what we've got." He put the vials inside some machine that whirred loudly as it spun them at high speed.

She felt perfectly fine. Just tired. Hopping down off the gurney, she turned to Devlin who was leaning on

the wall beside the door. "Wait and see. You heard it first."

Her smile slipped off her face when the corners of his mouth dipped even lower. "Put a rush on it. I want results by the morning."

"Will do."

"Come on, babe. You've gotta eat somethin'." Dev pushed the door open for her.

"You cooking?"

"Fuck, no." He put his arm around her, his palm landing on her hip.

A buzz of electricity fanned out from the contact. She stepped away, a subtle reminder to herself that she couldn't have that kind of connection, more than it was a message to him. "Who, then?"

He shoved his hands in his back pockets, brow pulled tight. "Lock. Sometimes Sienna, or Margo, but she's out of action. Probably won't stop her, though."

The delicious scent of curry met them in the hallway, getting stronger as they neared the kitchen. How long had she been asleep for? "What is the time?"

"'Bout eight p.m."

She trailed behind him over to the island bench across from where Margo was filling several plates with rice and the creamy orange curry. Her hair was now bright yellow.

"I slept for fourteen hours?" Shiloh's stomach let out a whine rather than a rumble. "No wonder I'm hungry."

"Try thirty-eight."

Her head snapped up. "Thirty-eight hours!?"

"Yup." He pulled out a stool and lifted her onto it.

Margo huffed a laugh. "We wondered if you were dead."

Ouch.

Devlin's shoulders bunched as he sent Margo a look loaded with the power of ten atomic bombs.

She tilted her head, a lopsided smirk playing on her features. "Oh, come on. It's a little bit funny. We've all gotta die from something."

His eyebrows dipped so low, his eyes looked like two black pits under their shadow. Nostrils flaring, he ripped a packet of cigarettes from his back pocket before stalking off.

"That vampire has no sense of humor." Margo shook her head and put a steaming plate of food in front of Shiloh, handing her some silverware. "Dig in."

"Thank you." She scooped up some curry and dug into the rice, loading her fork before blowing on the food. "How is your leg?"

"Almost better." Margo held up a cane. "Just need a bit of help from my trusty friend. Vampire blood is a cure-all."

Shiloh nodded, remembering how it had mended her broken arm. And how Sienna's blood had saved Devlin's life. There were no miracle cures available to Shiloh now.

Taking her first bite, she savored the flavor on her tongue: the mix of spices and cream with the fluffy rice and the meat melting in her mouth. It was unlike anything she'd ever tasted.

What's different? She looked down at her plate, stabbing a piece of meat and slicing it in half. *Oh, it's raw.* Juices from the meat seeped into the curry sauce, marbling veins of red through the orange. *Mm, just how I like it.* Her jaw froze, mid-chew. "Am I going to die if I ingest animal blood?"

"Animal blood doesn't affect us. It's as potent as water, unfortunately."

Oh, good. I suppose.

She cleared her throat and made an attempt at small talk. "So how long have you worked for Devlin?"

"Only since he came back to Cali. The time before that, I was with him for ten years in San Jose. Then one day, he up and disappeared for nearly two centuries. And here we are, full circle."

"Two centuries? How old are you?" Shiloh shoved the food in her mouth, relishing the heavenly sustenance.

"Three hundred, give or take a few decades."

"Mostly give." Zain interrupted them, coming in from the hallway and piling two plates with food.

"Watch it, smart-ass." Margo grabbed a dish towel by one corner, spun it, and whipped it at the back of his legs.

He hopped on his toes, trying to get away. "Ow. That stings."

"So did your comment, baby boy." She threw the towel back on the dish rack, grinning at Shiloh. "Zain is a newborn. It's only been six months since he dug himself out."

Two months longer than me. I wonder how old Devlin is.

"Any dessert tonight, Mags?" Zain balanced the plates on one arm while grabbing two bits of naan bread.

"Not after you insulted me."

"Aw, come on." His words were muffled around a piece of bread.

"Tell Lock I made him an apple pie."

"Sweet." Zain's eyes lit up like a Christmas tree.

"It's for him, not you. You can kiss my ass."

"That cuts me deep." He grinned, before ripping off another chunk of naan with his teeth.

"Aren't you supposed to be on control room duty with Lock? Get out of my kitchen."

"*Your* kitchen?"

"It's mine tonight." She threw the retort at his back as he left. Margo shook her head, laughing. "Kids. Who'd have them?"

All Shiloh's questions came rushing to the tip of her tongue. She lined them up, deciding to take it one at a time. "Can vampires have children?"

"God, no. The ability to procreate dies with our humanity. In my opinion, that's a good thing, but if you ask Sienna, she'll disagree. Can you imagine breastfeeding? Ouch."

Er, no. Shiloh swallowed twice. She'd be turning seventeen in two weeks. Any thought of having babies had been *waaay* down the track. But with the option being wiped from the table, she suddenly had a knot in her throat, and the silence of her biological clock was more a pounding in her ears. "True. What else can't we do?" Shiloh searched the cupboards to find a glass, desperate for a drink.

"Here." Margo opened one of the cupboards above the bench beside the refrigerators and handed Shiloh a tumbler. "There's a dispenser on the fridge door."

"Thanks." Shiloh poured her drink and made her way back to her seat.

"We can't fly—total bummer—but there's not much we can't do. We're stronger and faster than humans." Margo sat on the stool beside Shiloh, resting her cane against the bench. "You were a swimmer, right?"

"Yeah."

"So, you could probably swim across the Pacific without getting a cramp. Your strength and endurance

are enhanced now. Or would be if you could feed." Her lips turned down. "Sorry for the reminder."

"It's okay."

"We have powers of persuasion over humans, and over those that we sire and regularly feed. It's not our instinct to feed from one vampire unless they're our intended mate. Vampires are notorious for drinking around." She grinned, flashing two sharp canines. "Our true mate would never control us in that way because it hurts them, too."

"In what way?"

"When vampires—true mates—bond, there's a splitting of the soul. A small part of one soul attaches to the other, and vice versa. Anything your mate does to hurt you, will also hurt them. Instant karma, baby. It's like you're one person almost. If one dies, the other one follows."

"Sounds intense."

"Shitty design flaw, if you ask me. That's why a lot of vampires choose to ignore the pull to partner up. It doesn't work that way if you are bonded by someone who isn't your true mate. They steal a part of your soul, but don't give any of theirs back. That's why Jax can drink and you can't. That's why if you die, he won't. But if he dies, you will."

Shiloh's eyes grew impossibly wide. *He has a piece of my soul. The pull I feel towards him—it's not him I'm drawn to. It's my soul trying to come back together.* That day in the parking lot. The reason she broke her arm. He'd already bonded with her. How many

times had he done this? How many had died because of his twisted game? How many more unstable minds were acting out the same script?

How long did she have until her time ran out?

"So any psycho vampire can run around biting and bonding random victims, condemning them to die?"

"Yes."

"That's insane."

"It keeps the population in check."

Shiloh's chin dropped as she looked at Margo. *Christ, what a heartless comment.*

"What? It does." She shrugged her shoulders. "Anything else you want to know?"

She might be thoughtless, but she was an open book. Shiloh was going to take advantage of that while she could. "How do vampires bond? I mean, it's not just sex, is it?"

"No. It happens when a chemical is released by the brain into the bloodstream and injected into your intended through a bite, *and* through sexual intercourse. It never happens by accident. If the intended isn't a willing recipient, their body will reject it."

"What if you think you're true mates, but it turns out you're not and it's too late?"

"Then you're screwed in an unhappy partnership for life, or one of you will die—the one who accepted the bond from the other."

No divorce for vampires. They'd want to be damn sure they'd found the one. How could Devlin be sure Shiloh was his true mate?

"You said you've worked for Devlin before. Two hundred years ago."

"Yes."

Shiloh swirled her bread in the bloody curry sauce, making patterns. "Why did he disappear?"

"I have no idea. That's a question you're going to have to ask him." Margo pushed her stool back and stood.

Skin prickling, Shiloh panicked. "Wait." Her first chance at getting any answers was about to walk off. "Devlin told me that he hadn't been reborn. He's definitely a vampire, so how is that possible?"

The corner of Margo's lips crept up until her smile was resplendent. "Magic." Her eyes flicked to somewhere behind Shiloh. "He's one of a kind." She knocked once on the countertop and moved towards the door. "I'll catch you later."

"Thanks for dinner. And the talk."

"You're welcome."

Margo ducked out of sight just as Devlin's hands landed on the bench either side of Shiloh. His warm breath fanned across her neck. "How's the food?"

The food was tasty, but his scent was better, intensified even more by the smoke. "Yummy." She

leaned away, stretching the space between them and reconstructing an invisible barrier. "You okay?"

Devlin backed up and moved beside her, crossing his arms. "She pissed me off."

"I figured."

"It took half a millennium for you to show and she makes a wisecrack about you dying on the first night? It ain't a fucking joke."

Her head spun so fast her neck cracked.

Five hundred years?

The cold war, civil war, the pilgrims arriving— he'd experienced eras that she'd only ever read about in books. She felt an inexplicable hollow in her chest at her exclusion from so many years of his life.

He'd suffered an eternity.

As she stared, the ghosts of years spent waiting for her haunted his eyes. The torture he'd endured, knowing his mate was unquestionably unobtainable, was an armor of pain for all to see. Then it hit her. It wasn't possible for Shiloh to experience the next five hundred years, whatever wonders and horrors that entailed. He'd waited so long, and his wish would never be fulfilled.

She rested her fork on the edge of her plate, not intending to pick it up again as her stomach pinned itself to her spine. "Did you ever wonder if you weren't meant to be bonded?"

His chest expanded before he dropped his chin and forced a breath out. "I didn't want it. I called bullshit

on the whole thing. But about seventeen years ago, I looked in the mirror and saw ya beside me. I knew you was comin' then."

"You saw me?"

"Your reflection. The way ya look now."

Oookay.

"Why didn't you come and find me sooner?"

"I told ya, I didn't want this. I knew my fate when I was born, and I wasn't fuckin' happy about it. You, being my mate? I knew it was a death sentence for you. I figured if I stayed away, you'd be safe." He dropped his arms and walked to the wall of windows, turning his back. "You deserved a normal life. You had dreams. Ain't no way I was messing with that. Salt Lake City was far enough away to divert danger. But I didn't keep a close enough watch. He knows how to block me. He got to you before I knew what he was doin'." Devlin turned to face her again, his jaw tight. "I made plans to come get you, but he found out somehow."

"You moved here around the time I was bitten, didn't you?"

"I arrived the same day."

"He knew."

"Yeah."

She pushed the plate away, the mouthwatering scent now sour in her nose. Something still didn't add up. "What I don't get is why it took him so long to bite. We were together for over a year."

Devlin's eyes flashed red for a second and he closed them, pausing before he answered. "He couldn't bite you before you turned sixteen, for starters. But he needed to be sure you'd accept his bond when he offered it. He needed to make you fall in love with him."

She clenched her teeth, trying to hold herself together, but it didn't stop the waterfall of anguish pouring from her eyes. *Oh, God.* What the fuck had she done to deserve this? How had she not known something was off? *How could I be so stupid?*

Devlin lifted her off the stool, cradling her in his arms. This solid man held her like she was an offering from God. How could she trust him when she'd been so thoroughly screwed over before? Because she just knew. *And didn't I ignore all those niggling feelings?* When Jax had been so insistent on getting in her panties and she'd given in. When he'd started climbing in the window and she'd let him. Fucking stupid. She'd lost herself in order to please him. The devil.

Was Devlin asking anything of her? He was asking her to trust her gut. He wanted her to be safe. To stay alive long enough for him to figure out a plan.

Shiloh's tears slowed, soothed by the rhythmic rocking of her body against his as he took them out of the kitchen and down the hallway. Whatever Jax had taken from her, she felt like Devlin had the power to give it back. If only there was a chance that she'd survive. She needed God to grant her a miracle. Wrapped in the blanket of Devlin's power that surged with every beat of his heart, anything seemed possible.

She sat up, finally noticing where they were headed, and her pulse jumped at the thought. "We aren't going where I think we are. Devlin, no."

Carrying her through the billiards room and gymnasium, he paused at the doors to the pool area. Her body stiffened in his arms. He murmured in her ear, "Relax. I ain't gonna make you go in the water."

"Can I get down now?"

"No," he replied. She squirmed, but he put a stop to her defiance with his lips on hers. "Don't. I saw your face after you got back in the pool. You won, babe. That was your Olympics, right there. I ain't letting that fucker take that away again."

Shiloh's body stilled as his words filtered through. Her brief moment of triumph played on her mind. She'd broken the lock Jax had put on her fear. Did she really want to play the victim for the short amount of time she had left? Hadn't he taken enough?

Devlin nodded at the doors and they swung open.

"How do you do that?"

"The doors know I'm boss."

"You can speak to inanimate objects now?" She couldn't hide the sarcasm in her voice.

"I can command most things. I tried to remove the bullet outta my shoulder while I waited for you, but I fucked up. Severed an artery or somethin'."

She gulped at the memory of all that blood as it aroused her hunger and pricked her fears. But a bigger

dilemma eclipsed her reaction. If he had power over things, why hadn't he ended Jax before she'd gotten involved? Why hadn't he crushed the soul-stealing leech to dust?

She didn't get to voice her question before he'd put her on a chair and stripped off his shirt and jeans. The fabric wiped her brain clean as it fell to the tiles. She didn't think she'd ever get used to seeing his exposed form in all his sinewy strength. At least he had underwear on. Although, she almost wished he didn't.

She stared at his back as he sat on the edge of the pool before easing into the water. Hidden partially by his long hair, freckles scattered dark patterns on each shoulder. He disappeared under the surface, but her eyes remained fixed on the spot where he'd been, a freeze frame of those beautiful imperfections on her brain. In her imagination, she'd already extended her tongue to lick them. Shiloh had to clamp her teeth together to stop her flesh from following suit.

Shiloh and Devlin's connection was a living breathing being in its own right. Even against insurmountable odds, it would not be denied.

It doesn't even matter. She couldn't do a damn thing about it. Insurmountable odds would win in the end.

He treaded water in the center of the pool, the lights reflecting off the contours of his body. "Are ya getting in or not?"

She had to clamp her eyes shut. "I'm not wearing a suit."

"Neither am I."

Believe me, I know.

Shiloh bit her lip, thinking she was insane for even contemplating getting in after the dark shadow he'd cast over her first attempted return. But he was right. That cool liquid was her happy place. If he'd delivered his revelation while she'd been in bed, would that mean she'd never sleep there again? No. Shiloh needed to sever the association she'd formed between the pool and tragedy. If anything could do the job, it was the allure of his mostly naked form under the surface, and his beckoning eyes.

He'd discarded his clothes like it was no biggie. Could she do the same? *Which underwear did I put on?* White lace wouldn't have been such a good idea—but black cotton, that was passable. Luckily, she'd gone for conservative after her shower. It wasn't like he hadn't seen her in a swimsuit before. A black bra and panties were pretty much the same, right?

"Turn around. I'm not giving you a strip show."

His shoulders jerked with a shrug before he complied. "Whatever you say."

She spun away and undressed, peeking over her shoulder to make sure he wasn't looking. His arms moved in slow circles, keeping him afloat, but other than that, he wasn't budging. She slipped into the water behind him and kicked her way to the deep end.

He still didn't turn.

"You can look now."

"I know." Instead of facing her, he sank under the surface before bobbing back up and rolling into a float. "Why do ya like the water so much?"

"In the water is where I excel; why wouldn't I love it? It tests me repeatedly, and I push my limits until I do better."

"You ain't reached your full potential yet."

And I won't. Not now. She didn't voice her thoughts. What was the point? Besides, her throat was too tight to let anything pass. Silence hung like a noose between them.

"I never liked swimming much."

She blinked as his words brought her mind back to the present. "Why?"

"It reminds me of being in my mother's womb."

What? She narrowed her eyes at his floating form, his hair like a cloud of ink in the water. "You remember?"

"Everything."

That's not normal. Nobody remembers that. What the hell is he?

Her heartbeat sounded a staccato as she reached for purchase on the tiled edge. "You weren't born human, were you?"

"No." He flipped over and swam to the shallow end, pulling himself to sit on the side of the pool. "I don't mean to scare ya. I wanna tell you the truth. What I am. I

ain't gonna hurt you. If I had my way, you'd be home with your family, and we'd have never met."

"You said that you weren't *re*-born. What are you?" Her words came on shortened breath, but he heard them well enough to answer.

"There ain't no word for it."

"What does that mean?"

"All I know is, my mam was a Lilin. The daughter of Lilith and the angel of death, Archangel Samael. And my father was an ancient vampire. The first vampire. The virus that causes humans to turn, it started with him. But I got the virus through his genes, not a bite. I got no clue how he fathered me. There ain't been no vampire babies since, and the virus kills children. You gotta be at least sixteen. So I guess I'm somethin' else."

Yes, you are.

Shiloh didn't think it was possible for his eyes to get any blacker, but they did.

She followed his lead, not moving, not saying anything, while inside her neurons were firing off all sorts of warning signals and justifications.

His grandfather was the grim reaper. His mother was a Lilin—the daughter of Lilith. Wasn't she a demon? His father sired the entire vampire race. *What. The. Fuck?*

If she hadn't seen Devlin's power—felt it engulf her—she wouldn't have believed him.

He sat before her, flesh and blood, watching . . .

She didn't bother hiding her shock—her galloping heart, her white knuckles. They both knew he'd dropped a bomb.

He was a mix of heaven and hell.

The vengeful side of heaven.

The seductive side of hell.

This was the match fate had chosen for her?

Why? Why me? How am I in any way his equal?

And how is he possible?

"My mother told me I was gifted from the gods. I was born to end the spread of the virus. I carry it, but I can't pass it on. I don't know how it's possible, but apparently throwin' a Lilin into the mix changes shit up." He shrugged, one side of his mouth quirking. "I'm a fucked-up crossbreed."

"Don't say that."

"Why not? It's the truth, ain't it? I'm the first and last of my race. My parents weren't s'posed to be able to bear children, but here I am. I feed on blood, but didn't go through no turnin'. I ain't never turned a human. I couldn't, even if I wanted to. I've killed plenty of 'em. The hunt gets me high." His eyes flashed red as his chest expanded. "I got powers that can crush a person's skull without me touching them. You got shafted when they paired us up."

Was he trying to scare her? Or make her feel better about the fact they'd never be together? She was in

a pool—the surroundings similar to the scene of her death—and yet she felt safer than she ever had.

"You offered me and my family protection. You helped me save my sister. I don't believe you're all bad."

"I'm the reason you need protection. They killed my mother when they found out about me. Burned her at the stake. My aunt hid me away. When she died, I came to the US. I been at death's door more times than I can count. The people who tried to end me have paid for what they did. All bar one."

He growled his last statement. A storm rolled across his features, casting the sharp angles in shadows as a wave of water barreled towards her. She ducked under the surface just before the small tsunami hit, splashing over the side of the pool and flooding the area.

Whoa. She stared wide-eyed at the carnage of strewn deck chairs and toppled planter boxes.

"Fuck." Devlin's curse echoed around the room.

Spinning around, Shiloh found Devlin glaring at the mess. She swam towards him, taking her time as he watched her, caution in his guarded gaze. Standing when she got to the shallow end, with the water now barely up to her thighs, she pushed through the field of energy still vibrating around him. "When you say they paired us up, what do you mean exactly? Who's they?"

"Heaven. My mother said my birth was predestined. That I was s'posed to lead a new race. More powerful than vampires. Eventually, they'd cease to exist and there'd be no need for humans to die no more. We can't turn 'em and we can't use their blood. I need

vampire blood to feed, for now, until another of my kind is created. Forming a bond with my true mate was supposed to continue the race and unleash my full power."

"Your full power?" *There's more?*

"Yeah. I ain't sure what she meant by that. But a shit ton of vampires don't wanna see that happen."

"Jax."

"He's at the front of a long line."

"You're fighting a war on your own. The people on your team are the enemy. *I'm* the enemy."

"I got no intentions of wiping out the vampire population. I need them to survive." He rubbed a thumb across his stubble. "I gotta stop assholes like Jax doin' what he did to you. That ain't right. Stealing souls. Turning a human is one thing. Keeping a piece of their soul prisoner, that's another."

It *was* evil. There was no pretty way to spin that twisted shit. She shuddered before going over what he'd said, sorting it all out in her mind. "You can't change humans into vampires, and you can't drink human blood. So if you'd come to me when I was human, we wouldn't have been able to be together anyway."

"No."

"Did you—" Her throat clamped shut as tears pricked her eyes. She took a minute. "Did you *let* . . . him bite me?"

"Yes." He stared at her under heavy brows, eyes as black as night.

She choked.

"It was the only way. He would've killed you and left you to rot if I had tried to stop it. I was s'posed to stop the bond. You responded to me . . . in the coffee house, but he blocked me. I dunno how."

"We need to find out how. If we do, maybe we can stop him."

Footsteps splashed through the puddle of water near the entry. "Uh, boss?" Lock entered, the tension in his body an entity of its own, weighing heavy in the air.

Shiloh backed towards Devlin, crossing her arms over her chest.

"Later, Lock." Devlin almost growled.

The man held up a cell phone. *Shiloh's* cell phone. "We got comms."

"Who from?"

"Jax."

Dread poured its heft into Shiloh's limbs.

"He's got the sister."

No! No, no, no, no.

Shiloh's gut hollowed out as Devlin's arms clamped around her. He bellowed out a roar that rattled the windows and blew Shiloh's hair forward to cover her face. She clapped her hands over her ears and wrenched out of his hold.

Shoving to his feet so fast the tiles cracked under the pressure, his eyes burned with fire from the pits of hell and his voice sank to match. "He's gonna wish he was dead."

Chapter

Eight

Defection

Lanie released a hacking cough, her esophagus burning as something hard was pulled out of her mouth. Sifting through the fog in her mind, she fought against her heavy eyelids, trying to pry them open. *Wha—? Ugh. What's going on?* Patches of light and shadow filtered through her stubborn lids. Unrelenting electronic beeps speared the quiet. Bitter plastic coated her tongue and nostrils. She searched her brain for feedback from the rest of her body. The reply was a suspended pause. The fog had infiltrated her flesh, diminishing her capacity to move, or feel.

The beeping stopped. A rush of cool air accompanied the removal of a weight covering her. Dull

objects glanced off her skin, as though she was wearing a padded suit, their touch barely alighting her nerve endings. She was flipped forward and bent over a hard object, before falling backwards into an awkward landing. Unable to control her movements, she was as useful as a puppet. But her body was folded in two. She knew that much. Her lungs couldn't expand properly. One nostril was blocked by the pressure of her kneecap.

Wherever Lanie was stuffed, it started to move, the squeak of wheels coming from underneath her. With her cognition muted she couldn't garner any fight or appropriate response. But somewhere deep inside, she was screaming. Sweat beaded on her lip, making her face slip to the side of her knee and freeing her airway a little more.

It still wasn't enough.

Her consciousness slipped in and out of darkness, unable to keep its hold on reality.

———

"Lanie, my love. You're finally awake."

She blinked her eyes, a wood-paneled wall filling her blurred vision. *Where am I?* Groaning at the cacophony of aches as she rolled to her back, Lanie cursed herself for moving.

That voice is familiar. What is that smell?

"I've made you some soup. You must be starving." Seth's face came into view, a beautiful smile in place. "Hi, Sleeping Beauty."

Her vision warped in and out of focus, but she had a perfect picture of him in her mind. *He's so freakin' gorgeous.* "Hi," she croaked. "Where's Shiloh?"

"Don't you remember?" He gave her a pitying look and helped her to sit up, packing cushions behind her back. "Oh, baby. Your memory has gone again. You haven't been the same since the accident."

Accident? He spooned some soup into her mouth. She sputtered, struggling to swallow the salty, hot broth.

"Shiloh blamed it on you. She said you grabbed the wheel. Your family kicked you out of home. I've been looking after you ever since." Stroking her face, he enchanted her with his kaleidoscopic eyes. "I'm so sorry, baby. It's just you and me now."

Her heart swelled at his declaration, euphoria flooding her veins. He offered another spoonful. She leaned forward to take it, wincing as pain shot through her head. "Thanks for taking care of me."

He frowned and put the bowl on the bedside table. "You're in pain. I'll get you your medication."

Her euphoria faded a little as he retreated through the door, and jumbled thoughts formed a confusing tapestry in her head. It made sense that she'd been kicked out of home. It was inevitable. But Shiloh and Seth were in love. Was it Lanie's fault they'd broken up? She groaned again, frustrated that she couldn't remember something so major.

"Here." He placed the pills in her palm and helped her raise them to her mouth, a glass of water at

the ready to wash them down. "There. You'll feel better again soon.

She stared at him over the rim of the glass. *Lucky me. I get to look at him all day.* "Where are we?"

"Shh, you're safe. You don't need to worry about that."

She frowned for a second as her mind tried to think, but she lost the trail, diverted towards gratitude. "I'm not worried."

"Good." He smiled again, lifting another spoonful of soup. "Finish all your dinner. We want you fully recovered by your birthday. Sweet sixteen." His eyes seemed to spark with flecks of red.

Mesmerizing. She stared as she swallowed down the liquid, not listening to what he was saying.

"I have big plans, baby. Big plans."

———

Bile burned the back of Shiloh's throat as her wet T-shirt dripped water down her bare legs. She hadn't had time to throw on her shorts and they were soaked from the tsunami anyway. *This can't be happening.* She pictured Lanie's beaten and bruised body lying in the hospital bed, tubes and wires snaking in a tangle of technology. Heard the hum and click of the machine breathing for her sister and the rhythmic beep of the monitor giving assurance of life.

How could Lanie have survived being unplugged from all of that?

"What did he say?" Devlin demanded as he stormed out of the billiards room, wrapping a towel around his waist, with Shiloh and Lock following.

"Checkmate."

Devlin's footsteps stopped abruptly, his fist pounding the wall to form a crater in the brick. "Fucker." Continuing his march, he flexed his hand. "Where's Sienna?"

"She's at the hospital. They called her."

Why didn't they call us? How could they have let this happen? A high-pitched ringing assaulted Shiloh's ears as images of a dead Lanie barraged her mind. Or worse. *Vampire Lanie.*

"Get her on the phone." Devlin slammed the flat of his palm into the air in front of him. The resulting pulse of energy swung open the door to the theatre room with a loud crack.

Shiloh bolted past him, thumping on the control room door. If they could tap into the city's CCTV, then surely they could access the hospital's security cameras.

Evren greeted her with a scowl, blocking her entry. "Staff only."

"Back the fuck up, Evren." Devlin loomed behind Shiloh, his breath hot on her neck.

"Gone soft." Ren moved back, pouting and muttering under her breath.

"You really wanna test me right now?" He swung a finger in her direction and she fell on her ass.

Lock passed Devlin a cell phone, giving Evren a sidelong look as he followed her to the desk.

"Sienna. How the fuck did he get through?" Devlin's fingers yanked at his hair, eyes fixed on the screen showing a deserted hospital room. "A fucking linen cart? You gotta be shitting me. Did you find the nurse?" Releasing his hair, his arm dropped by his side as his red eyes flicked to Shiloh's. "Dead." He pulled the phone away from his ear, the crunch of his teeth grinding together sending shivers down her spine. Stretching his neck side to side until it cracked, he screwed up his nose and sniffed before resuming the conversation. "Find him."

Passing the phone back to Lock, Devlin searched the screens again. "He mind-fucked a nurse to do the deed and put a bullet in the guy's brain on delivery of the package. Where's the footage?"

Another innocent life extinguished. Shiloh squatted down, leaning her back against the wall and squeezing her eyes shut. She didn't want to see after all. There'd been enough bloodshed and madness. If she watched her sister's lifeless body being carted away, she'd never be able to get the image out of her head.

"There. That door. I want the view outside that door."

"Okay, give me a sec."

Shiloh heard the play of Zain's fingers over the keyboard, thinking it sounded a lot like rain on a windshield. The last thing a person would hear before skidding out of control on a wet, stormy night.

"*Fuck* . . . wait. Back it up," Devlin barked.

Shiloh pushed her palms into her closed eyes, the temptation to open them almost overpowering her. Thank God the video had no sound. It was bad enough hearing the commentary.

"That ain't him holding the gun. He's got another vampire helping him. Added to the dead bodies in the yard and any humans he decides to screw with, and he has himself an army. How the fuck is he controlling so many? It ain't with blood."

"Money, probably." Evren weighed in. "Vampires are just as greedy as humans."

"Nah. He ain't got that much. People ain't gonna lay down their lives just for a piss-weak amount of dough. They do it to protect something they believe in, or fight for their right to it."

Shiloh uncovered her eyes, immediately caught in Devlin's gaze.

"He either threatened 'em or promised 'em something." He paused, still looking at her. "Power. Immortality . . . magic."

Moving towards her, his energy field encircled her with a magnetic pull before he took her hands and tugged her to her feet. "Evren, take Shiloh upstairs."

What? No. "Why can't I stay?"

Shiloh's question got lost underneath Evren's simultaneous protest. "You're sending me off to fucking babysit?" Her chair squealed as she swiveled to gape at his back.

Devlin didn't take his eyes off Shiloh. "Is there somethin' wrong with your hearing, Ren?"

"Naw, boss. We got you." Lock frowned at his girl with a subtle shake of his head.

"I'll take her," Zain offered.

His grip tightening around Shiloh's hands, Devlin twisted his head slowly to stare at the teen.

If she had to go anywhere with anyone other than Devlin, she'd rather it be with Zain. Even Lock would be better than Ren. But she didn't want to go at all.

She repeated her question. "Why do I have to go?"

Devlin released his hold and nodded his head at his IT guru. "It's safer this way."

Zain brushed past and held the door for her. "Shiloh, come on."

She hesitated, searching Devlin's black gaze for a shred of warmth.

Heaven and hell.

He turned away, taking the seat Zain had vacated.

Dismissed.

She felt a tug on her hand before her body followed through the exit. "Where are we going? What are they going to do?" Shiloh watched the flicker of changing screens over her shoulder before she lost sight through the narrowing crack in the door.

"They're going to track him. The sneaky bastard knows how to fly under the radar, but now he's got baggage." Zain's shoulders bunched and he snapped his gaze to hers. "Sorry. That sounded bad."

Her nose screwed up at his callous referral to her sister before he came to an abrupt stop, Shiloh bumping into his back. "What—"

"Wait here." Spinning on his heel, he jogged down the stairs, and stuck his head back in the control room. "Check the skies; he might have wings."

Eyebrows shooting up, Shiloh pictured Jax sprouting wings and carrying her sister off in his claws like a vulture with a prize carcass.

Zain caught up to her, a smirk on his face. "Not actual wings." He trotted past the rows of recliners facing the big-screen.

"Oh. You meant he might've taken a flight. But he would have had to hide Lanie." Her eyes widened as her body recoiled. "He's stuffed her in a suitcase. She's small enough. Oh, my God. She's going to die."

"Whoa. Stop. She's not gonna die. We'll get her back."

Shiloh halted, her nostrils flaring and anger rising to a boil in her blood. "You know what? I don't want to hear any more bullshit stories about how everything is going to be fine. How the fuck is anything fine?" Her voice gradually rose to ear-pounding levels. "My sister could already be dead, for all we know. And if not, she's at Jax's mercy. Is he going to bite her, too? What the hell does he want with her? Why do I have to lose everyone I

love?" She let out a growl at the unfairness of it all. The sound pierced everything within reach. The curtains lining the theatre room ripped from their fastenings. Yards of gray fabric dropped in piles, looking like the fortified walls of a bunker. All she needed to add was a topping of twisted barbed wire and she was ready for Jax's war. He wanted it? He was going to get it.

"Fuck me. Are you sure she's not part banshee?" Evren jiggled her finger in her ear, scowling at Shiloh from the control room door.

"Come on, Shiloh. Let's go." Zain tapped her on the elbow.

"I'm not leaving." Zeroing in on the goth, a pulse of energy started vibrating in Shiloh's tailbone. One more word from this bitch and the last thread of Shiloh's control would snap. She shifted her stance as the pressure in her back became uncomfortable.

"Aw, baby doesn't wanna sit in the corner." Ren sneered, her statement inciting a rage that burned Shiloh to the core.

A wave of power raced up her spine, juicing her muscles for attack. Releasing a hiss, Shiloh pounced, crossing the room in one move to knock Ren out cold with a punch. The pulses of energy kept coming, building and building until the air shimmered around her in oily ribbons like the heat rising off desert dunes.

Something was happening to her being. Something irrevocable. *God help me.*

"What the fuck?" Lock lurched into the room, following Devlin.

Dev slapped a palm out, stopping his friend from moving an inch. "Don't touch her."

A low rumble of thunder rolled out from Lock's chest. Ren moaned, dragging herself upright with awkward movements. Leaning on her arms, with her legs curled beside her, she stretched her jaw. "Fuck." Aiming eyes of crimson malice in Shiloh's direction, Ren stumbled to her feet and pitched her body at her target.

Grinding her teeth, Shiloh held both palms out in an unmistakable signal to back off.

Coming up against an invisible barrier, Ren's body twisted and fell. Growling, she tried again, looking like a mime the morning after a bender. "Cut the shit, D. Let me at her."

"I ain't doin' nothin'." Devlin smirked.

"Bullshit." Evren came at Shiloh again, bouncing off thin air.

Devlin growled at his sniper. "I ain't a fucking liar. Sit your ass down, you're embarrassing yourself."

Muscles convulsing, bones warping—each molecule somehow morphed to shed the bulk of Shiloh's humanity. The force of the change had her hovering an inch above the floor. She held in a cry of pain, focusing her attention on keeping this woman the hell away, rather than acknowledging the possibility that she was losing herself completely. "Leave me alone." The demand rumbled out as if demons plucked the fleshy harp of her voice box.

"What the fuck is going on, then?" the goth spat.

"It's her." Devlin's eyes lit up.

Ren's head swiveled back to Shiloh. "What about her?"

Devlin looked at Shiloh, his face stretched in elation, gaze glowing like a beacon guiding her home. "She found her power. Fuck, yeah."

As soon as the words left his mouth, Shiloh reconnected with the floor. Energy draining through the soles of her feet, her body collapsed just as the curtains had. Managing choppy gasps of air between clenched teeth, she whimpered at the horrible realization—*I can't see.* Her hearing filtered through a tunnel lined in cotton wool. She was able to grab words here and there—*Shock. Myles. Med room*—and then . . . nothing.

Chapter

Nine

Suspicious

Lanie propped herself up against the pillows, head pounding like it'd been stuck between clashing cymbals for hours. It was dark outside, from what she could tell. There was only one window across the small room. The glass was covered with aluminum foil behind a heavy, woven curtain. If not for a small tear in the foil, she wouldn't have had any visual marker of time, the break leaking in a fine beam of light just visible through the weave early in the morning. The other clue to the time was the intermittent song of a mockingbird chirping through the most popular bird mating calls. Fucking thing wouldn't shut up.

She stared at the pills in a cup beside the bed. Seth had left them there before leaving. He told her he'd be back soon and to take them if she had pain. Pain was her constant. The houseguest that needed a place to crash for 'a few days' and never left. Yeah, she could swallow the pills and retreat into numbness again, but they always knocked her out. She'd barely been awake for days. It could've been weeks. Who the fuck knew?

Seth did.

Where did he go? I need to pee.

She slapped a palm on her thigh, tightening her lips because she'd barely felt a sting. It was like her legs were made of rubber. Useless appendages. For decorative purposes only. They moved sometimes, but not where she wanted them to go, and never much more than a twitch or a shudder. She was working on it. Whenever she was conscious.

I refuse to cry.

Flaring her nostrils, she clamped her eyelids shut and dragged in a breath.

I seriously need to pee.

At least she still had bladder control.

Where is he?

Through narrowed eyes, she estimated the distance to the door and the height of the bed. Letting out a sigh, she figured she didn't have a choice. She'd have to drag herself to the bathroom. She tipped her shoulders to the side, reaching towards the floor. Both hands flat on the carpet, she walked them slowly forward as the blood

rushed to her head, amplifying the percussion section between her ears.

Fuck. Maybe I should've had the damn pills.

Gritting her teeth, she looked back as her legs slid towards the edge of the mattress. Bracing her arms, she waited for the thud. One. Two. *Ooh, I think I felt that.* Dust teased a sneeze from her nose. *Goddamn, Seth, would it kill you to vacuum?*

Where was he?

Digging her elbows into the plush pile, she inched forward.

How could he leave me like this?

Crash, clang—the cymbals continued their barrage as her pulse drummed a beat behind her temples. She sneezed again, wondering if her head would explode before her bladder did. Another two feet and she'd be at the door. Left, right. Twelve more inches. She lifted her arm to grab the handle. *Too far.* Shuffling her butt closer to the door, she straightened up her torso and reached again. *Shit.* She'd never be able to reach the door handle. Either this place was designed by giants, or she was too much of a short-ass.

He said he'd take care of me. That he'd never leave me. Where the fuck is he now, huh? Why were they together? She wasn't even sure if they liked each other.

That was it. She couldn't hold it any longer. The discomfort in her bladder suddenly eased off and she looked down as a wet patch soaked her shorts. Biting her

lip, she swiped at the renegade tear defiantly trailing down her cheek. *Fuck it. Fuck this. And fuck him.*

Throwing up a middle finger, she aimed it at the exit, fully prepared to hold the pose until Seth copped an eyeful of her dissatisfaction.

She didn't have to wait long.

She heard a key rattle the handle before a click. *The door was locked? Why was the door locked?* Watching the handle turn, she knew her body was blocking the door from swinging open but was unable to move fast enough to prevent the collision.

Whack. Her side caught the brunt of the force. *Ouch.*

"Lanie!" Seth snapped as he poked his head through the gap. "What are you doing out of bed?"

She glared at him, finger still raised.

His face screwed up. "Did you piss yourself?"

"Well done, genius, you figured it out."

His eyes snapped to hers. She could've sworn they blazed red for a second before simmering to a shade of amber. *What was that?* He paused, smoothing out his features.

A feeling of bliss filtered through her system. The cacophony in her head hushed. She dropped her arm, finding it hard to remember why she'd had it up in the first place. *Oh, he is gorgeous. And he's all mine.* "Sorry about the mess. I tried to get to the bathroom."

He smiled, but it didn't quite reach his eyes. "I know, baby. I'm sorry I wasn't back in time."

"Where'd you go?"

"Out." His brow tightened as he dropped his gaze. "I'll get a towel."

"Thanks." He disappeared and she started to worry that he wasn't coming back, the bliss fading a little as if he'd taken it with him. "Seth?"

Silence.

Her mouth dried to a crisp. "Seth?" She raised her voice, shuffling her body to the side and out of the way of the door, exposing the full extent of her disgrace. *Oh. He's gonna be angry.*

The door swung open before he dumped a towel in her lap. "Here, clean yourself up." Shoulders bunched, he turned away, leaving her again.

"Um, I might need a bit of help."

His steps halted, his shoulders dropping. The euphoric wave she'd been riding since his return seemed to ebb. Slowly turning, he smiled. "Of course." Hooking his elbows under her armpits, he dragged her backwards and into the small bathroom, lifting her into the bath. "Yell when you're done. I'll have your pills ready." He shut the door behind him, the snap restoring the percussion section in her head.

She groaned and sneered at her wet pants and rubber legs. *Pathetic.* Crippled. Why would a guy like him want to be with her?

Grinding her teeth, she ordered herself to stop as something in her clicked. Her eyes narrowed at the door. Why *was* he with her? Shiloh loved him. There was no way Lanie would betray her sister by stealing her boyfriend away. What were the two of them doing holed up in this shoebox? Why was he so insistent on the pills?

Lanie managed to strip off her pants, leaving her top on in case he barged in. She put the towel off to the side for later. Sucking in a breath as cold water spurted from the faucet, she shivered. The liquid level rose along with her anger, wiping away the illusion she'd been under. Every time he was near, it was like he'd drugged her. The words of love he spouted didn't match his actions. Seth was full of shit. She'd always thought that, hadn't she?

What am I going to do now?

Passing the soap over her arm, she froze. In the crook of her elbow there was a small bruise surrounding a tiny puncture wound.

What. The. Fuck?

It could have been from when she was in hospital. No, it looked too fresh. Goosebumps paraded in the wake of the suds as her throat constricted.

Jesus, I think I'm in big trouble. Is he drugging me?

One thing was for sure: she wouldn't be swallowing any more of his brand of medicine.

"Hey, baby, are you done?"

Shit. "Just a sec."

After pulling out the plug, she grabbed the towel and covered herself as best she could, waiting for the water to drain completely. Calling him in, she put on a grateful smile despite the dread simmering in her gut.

He grinned at her, his eyes trailing over her towel. Something crawled along her skin, poking and prodding in a bid to get beneath her guard. Its sweet flavor teased her lips. She recognized it as the blissful rush he always induced in her. She glued her smile in place, determined not to let it slip, and hoping she could stop whatever he was doing by sheer will alone.

He scooped her out of the tub. "Let's get you back to bed."

"Um, do you mind if I try sitting up on the sofa for a change?" She forced herself to look him in the eyes. "Do we have a sofa?"

"But baby, you're not well enough, and you need to have your pills."

"But—"

"Nope. Doctor's orders."

"Is the doctor coming any time soon?"

"The doc knows you're in good hands. I'm looking after you, aren't I?"

"Yeah, baby . . ." *Ugh*, she imagined cutting out her tongue after its misuse of the endearment. ". . . you're doing a great job. I'd be lost without you." That was the sort of shit Shiloh used to say to him, wasn't it? Lanie hoped her act would pass. She could always blame

her behavior on the headache that continued to pummel her brain.

"Yes, you would." His eyes flared, his smile tainted with a sinister but subtle curl of his lip.

She held back a shiver. Whatever juju he was putting out still teased along her skin, its sweetness no longer a flavor she craved. It didn't sink under her defenses. Maybe because she was aware of it now. Did he know that she knew? She glanced at his eyes, but he was focused on where they were going.

Placing her back on the bed, he gathered some clothes from the dresser. "Here, you can put these on." After dropping the garments beside her, he took the glass of water and pills, and waved them under her nose. "Swallow. You know how to do that, don't you, baby?"

His laugh made her want to punch him in the cock.

Fucker.

Throwing the pills in her mouth, she grabbed the glass, took a swig, and tossed her head back.

"Good girl."

She sneered at his back, waiting until he'd locked the door before spitting the medicine out. Crushing it under the weight of the glass of water, she then sprinkled it on the carpet under the bed. After dressing in the shorts and shirt he'd given her, she rearranged her legs until she was comfortable.

Blinking back tears, she stared at the ceiling, absorbing the realization that she might be trapped. And

if so, her body was in no shape to perform an escape. She only hoped that clearing the drugs from her system would get everything back to normal.

What the hell had happened to her family? Where was Shiloh?

What was Seth planning?

For the first time in her life, Lanie prayed.

Please help me.

———

"How's your head?" Myles took the ice pack from Shiloh's temple, repositioning it as the blood pressure machine squeezed her bicep until the blood flow cut off.

"Myles?" The scent of hospital-strength disinfectant lingered in the exam room. She squinted, adjusting to the bright light reflecting off the white tiles. "What happened this time?"

"You had some sort of an episode brought on by stress and exhaustion. I'm keeping you in for observation for a few hours. I'll give you a mild sedative later tonight so you can catch up on much-needed sleep."

All she heard was "blah, blah, blah" as everything came flooding back. Knocking Evren down. The curtains. Devlin casting her out. "Lanie!" She wrenched her body upright. "Have they found her?"

"Whoa, lie down." He tried to place his palms on her shoulders, but only managed to hover above her, brow furrowed and arms straining. "Uh, can you try to relax?"

She pulled back the sheet, kicking her legs off the side of the gurney, ready to leap. "Have they found her?"

"No. Not yet." He shook his head.

After jumping down, she swayed on her feet for a second before grabbing onto Myles to steady herself. Her head and neck felt like they'd been replaced with a watermelon on a bendy straw. "Ugh. I feel weird."

"You need to rest. Lie down."

She plonked her butt back on the mattress and laid down before Myles adjusted the sheet over her bare legs. Shiloh's eyes were drawn to the corner of the room, finding Zain sleeping in a chair, his body slumped to one side. "Has he been there the whole time?" *Devlin sent a minder?*

"Yes."

"What about Devlin? Where is he?"

Myles adjusted his glasses. "Out looking for your sister."

"Hmph." She ground her teeth, still pissed that she'd been ordered out. Why couldn't she help? What was Devlin hiding?

"Zain." The doctor tapped the boy on the knee.

Flailing, Zain slid off the chair. "What, what?" He pushed the heels of his hands into his eyes before squinting at Shiloh. "Hey."

"Hey." Her tone was flat. "Are you on babysitting duty?"

"Nah. I'm just hangin' out."

Uh-huh. "Don't let me keep you up."

"You weren't. I was asleep."

"Right."

Stretching, with a yawn, he looked at Myles. "Is she good to go, Doc?"

"No. She'll be here for a little while longer."

"Oh." His brow scrunched as he looked her over before turning back to Myles. "Okay if I stick around?"

Shiloh answered, "Don't you have to? Isn't that what babysitters do?"

The doctor cleared his throat before sitting at the bench to scribble something in a file.

Zain's mouth twisted, his eyes darting to the door and back. "Myles is the one looking after you. I just thought you might want some company when you woke up, that's all. If you don't want me here, I've got plenty of other things I can be doing."

Oh, God. He'd been nothing but nice to her and she was snapping like a bitch. She was turning into Lanie. A rueful smile touched her lips. *Damn, I miss her.* Understanding her sister was like descending a staircase, one step after another, deeper under the ornery surface. Lanie must've felt cornered, misunderstood, out of control. Shiloh got it. She got why Lanie had put up walls. Why she bared her teeth and spat profanities, warning the world to back the fuck up.

But Shiloh also knew that there was never a good excuse for being an asshole. Whatever the world hurled

in your direction, you had the power to rise above it. If you started slinging shit around, it would always boomerang back to you. Sometimes you had to be the bigger person. Walk away. Make the choice to break the cycle. And sometimes it was necessary to trust. It was okay to accept help.

And Zain . . . there was something about him.

One thing was for sure: she needed to apologize. Heat flared across her face. "Sorry, Zain. It has been a big night."

"It's okay. I get it." He scratched his nose and sat back in his chair. "So, you've got a fierce haymaker punch, huh?" His lip ring glinted in the light as he grinned.

"I hit her, didn't I?"

"Yeah, you did." He sang his answer as if he relished the taste of it on his tongue.

"She's going to kick my ass now, isn't she?"

"First chance she gets." He nodded slowly. "But I'd like to see her try. I don't know what happened in there, but something changed—" Chewing on his lip ring, he stopped speaking. His gaze flicked to Myles who was still scribbling. "I got a feeling she's no match for you anymore."

The doc cleared his throat again.

Zain raised his eyebrows before continuing. "So how you feeling?"

"Super." She exaggerated the 'S', her face reflecting her disbelief in her own bullshit.

Zain choked on a laugh, his eyes widening. "Okay then." He scratched his head, looking over at Myles for a second. "I guess you're stuck here for a while. Lucky I'm available to entertain you, because this place is as boring as shit." He took his phone from the bench, sliding his thumb across the screen. "Check this out. People tryna drive on icy roads." He could barely get the words out past his laughter. "Oh, man, I'm gonna split my intestine. It's so fucking funny." Dragging his chair closer, he positioned the screen so she could see.

She'd expected to see YouTube, but he had his memo app open. He'd written her a note:

Myles listening. Shh.

A couple of swipes later the video played, showing a group of people impersonating bowling pins. She had to pry her laughter through gritted teeth, her gaze piercing Zain's reflection in the phone's screen. What was he insinuating? *Was something happening to her that they didn't want her to know?*

She risked a glance at Myles. He didn't appear to be paying them any attention, but how could she believe appearances? How could she believe any of what was happening? Her throat cramped as her breath shortened. *I want off this crazy train.*

Keeping her eyes glued to the screen and her attention on the doctor, she willed him to leave the room. In her mind, she watched him walk out over and over. In each scenario, he ended up somewhere different: in the

kitchen, eating a bagel; taking a Maserati for a spin down the winding driveway; writing a research paper; setting a mouse trap; painting a self-portrait. She had no idea what he normally did with his time, but she wished he'd go and do anything other than sucking the oxygen out of the room.

Her eyelids burned with the need to blink, but her stare refused to budge. If she shifted her gaze, she'd fasten it on the doctor and tip him off to her suspicion. Or worse, harm him like she'd done to Ren.

Shock loosened her jaw as a fine crack appeared in the corner of the screen. Zain's eyes shot to hers before he yanked the phone away. She snapped her eyelids shut. *Fuck.*

"You're tired. Get some sleep." Zain pushed his chair back to where it had been and hooked his headphones over his ears, once again smiling at the screen. But she knew he wasn't watching the video. He didn't laugh. As she peered at him through narrowed eyes, his plastic grin remained pinned in place, his absent stare not moving a millimeter. Nope. His thoughts had been sucked into a black hole inside his head. The same place she feared she was headed.

There wasn't any chance of getting answers any time soon. She closed her eyes again. She'd just have to wait it out. Sooner or later, the doc would have to let her go.

Wouldn't he?

———

"I want to speak to every fucking person he's ever had contact with and tear apart every place he's been. I wanna know what paper he uses to wipe his ass. Get the kid to tap into all the fucking satellites if that's what it takes. And if that motherfucker is hiding in a hole, I'm gonna need a shitload of explosives." Devlin grunted as he strapped a pair of Glocks into holsters under each arm.

A pendant light hung low above a table covered in a buffet of assault weapons, while racks of them hugged the rock walls of the room. Automatic and semi-automatic guns, daggers, grenades—he even had access to chemical weapons. The black market provided them with everything they could want except the motherfucker they were after and his prisoner.

"What are you going to do? Blow the sister to smithereens, as well?" Sienna cocked a dark brow.

"Nah. I'm gonna find her first and let her light the fuse. If she's anything like her ancestors, she ain't gonna need a match or an invitation." He tested the feel of his hunting knife in his grip, the blade throwing light across his features.

"Who else knows about them?"

Sliding the knife back into its sheath, he cracked his neck. "Nobody."

"Keep it that way."

Was that a fucking order? Devlin ensnared his teammate with a stone-cold stare, her throat bobbing with a swallow. She'd been his 'inside man' in the

LAPD for decades, and warmed his body with hers whenever he'd needed for even longer.

But she regularly forgot her place.

He'd gotten a kick out of putting her back in it, behind closed doors. But now her smell was sickly sweet, her skin like cracked glass, marred with sharp edges that'd catch him out and leave a scar. He hadn't gone to her room since Shiloh had been reborn. He hadn't had anyone. He couldn't. And fuck him, it was screwing with his brain and his cock in the shittiest way.

Slipping the knife back out, he aimed the sharp point at Sienna's mouth, looking down the length of its blade. "If word gets out, it ain't gonna be from my tongue." He waited a second before lifting his gaze to hers, holding the warning until he saw a flicker of red in her eyes and a twitch of her lips.

Sienna should know how important this was. Shiloh couldn't know what she was.

Because if she did, she'd leave.

"We need more vampires. If he's got himself an army, I gotta match him fang for fang."

"That can be arranged."

"Just like that, huh? You think the vampires are gonna jump at the chance to fight for me? Their prophesied destroyer?"

"There's more support for you than you think. The word about Jax is getting around. He's killing fangs by the dozen every day and controlling many more. You're considered the lesser of two evils. They know

he's out for power and blood control. People are scared. They want protection. We can give it to them."

"How many of 'em are willing to fight for it? To die?"

"More than you know."

"I want 'em vetted. They don't pass all the tests—they don't get near us. Snap on a glove if ya gotta. If there's a whiff of Jax's shit up their asses, you know what to do."

"Yes, I do. Leave it to me."

He nodded and pulled a pack of smokes from his pocket, listening to the click of her heels as she marched away. "Sienna?"

She paused, pivoting on the spot. "Mm?"

"Thanks."

Her brows jumped, her mouth parting, but no words came. She clamped her lips shut and nodded, leaving the room.

Lighting up his cigarette, he took a deep drag and held it in for an endless minute. "Yeah, I'm an asshole." Smoke billowed around him as he released the statement of fact.

He *was* an asshole.

It's how I survive.

Chapter

Ten

Fuckery

"Make sure she gets back to her room safely." Handing Shiloh a small bottle, Myles focused his stern gaze on her. "Here. Take this before bed. It should settle you for the night. Come back and see me in the morning; I'd like to check you over again. If you don't come to me by nine, I'll come to you."

"Thanks."

"You're welcome."

Scooting off the gurney, she couldn't get to the exit fast enough.

Zain held the door open. "After you."

She rolled her eyes as she past him.

"Nice hospital gown. Um, you might want to hold the back closed or something."

Under the gown, she still wore the T-shirt she'd thrown on after her swim, although it was now dry. Cool air bit at the backs of her bare legs. She absentmindedly reached behind her to fix the problem, distracted by the thrill of energy coursing through her body. The soles of her feet hovered on a cushion of air that seemed to lift her higher with each step. Purposely planting each foot, she managed to ground herself. *Holy shit. I can float?* It was so tempting to test her newfound powers, but she somehow knew it was better to keep things under wraps.

What did this mean? Were Devlin's powers somehow transferring through their connection? But they weren't even bonded. Or was it something Jax was doing to her? Maybe the changes were some sort of evil voodoo and he was setting her up to be his weapon of destruction. *Oh, my God. What if he's still controlling me?*

I need to know more about Jax.

Zain sniffed, wiping his nose with the back of his hand. *Gross.* She pushed her disgust aside, tilting her head to watch him as a plan formed.

Shiloh lowered her voice. "Do you have a computer somewhere, apart from the control room?"

"Yeah, I have several. Why?"

She couldn't stop the grimace as she paused on the stairs.

Do I really want to drag him into this?

This is possibly the worst thing I've ever done.

Shit, shit, shit.

Damn it, I don't have a choice.

"Because I want you to help me search for info, and I don't want it to be tracked on my computer. I know they're watching me."

He lifted his chin, his chest expanding. "What are you searching for, because I can't go hacking into—"

"Shh. Relax. I want to know more about Jax. Why he took my sister. Why he used me. I deserve to know the truth. I think I can trust you. I can't trust any of the others. Not even Devlin because he wants to keep me in the dark. He knows what's going on. I should know, too."

Zain watched her under a scrunched brow.

He hadn't said no yet. That was a good sign. She figured she could push a little more. "Are there cameras in your room?"

"Yes, but I disabled them."

A devious smile spread across her face. "Let's go." She picked up her pace, taking two steps at a time.

He jogged to catch up. "Uh, I can't take you to my room."

"Why not?"

"D would cut off my balls."

Sucking both lips into her mouth she lowered her gaze to the floor, brainstorming a solution. She needed his help. "If I go in my room, have a shower, and pretend to go to sleep for about a half hour, will that give you enough time to loop the camera feed, so it looks legit?"

"What if he comes looking for you?"

She had no right to put Zain in this position. But wasn't he supposed to be babysitting her? What would it matter if Devlin found them together, surfing the internet? Even the weakest of justifications was enough for her to take the risk if it gave her any hope of saving her sister. *Sorry, Zain.* "I'll take my chances."

"I dunno. I like my balls attached."

"Please? I *need* to find her." Dead or alive, Lanie had to come home.

Zain let his eyelids fall as he caught his lip ring between his teeth. Threading his fingers, he put his hands on his head. "Ah, fuck. Okay, go. I'll give you forty minutes. Wait for my signal."

"Thank you." She didn't know what his signal was supposed to be, but she didn't wait around to find out either. He'd agreed to help her, and that was more than she could've hoped for.

After diving in and out of the shower, Shiloh tossed the covers over herself and turned on her side to face the door. Was he going to knock? No, they'd have cameras in the hallway, too. A text message? No, she didn't have her phone and they'd be tapped into that anyway. She thrashed her legs and rolled to her back,

forcing a breath out of her nose. Shit, she was supposed to be pretending to sleep.

She did her best to relax, her thoughts probing her deepest connection—her life-force.

Water.

Raindrops peppering her face.

Emerging from a bath, goosebumps erupting over her skin.

The cool rush of liquid over her tongue.

Water threading through her fingertips.

When she swam, she became so engrossed it was like she was one with the liquid medium. Like she could blend her molecules and get it to do whatever she wanted. It came to life, pushing her along as much as she dragged her body through it.

In a split second something changed. She was somewhere else. Someone else.

Her heart drummed a comfortably fast tempo, doubling the time of the booming bass beat from outside. Tranquility permeated the tiny space she was in. Water surrounded her, holding her buoyant. No, not water. It tasted salty and felt hot. She couldn't see anything, even when she peeled her eyes wide.

Squeezed in as she was, her arms and legs had little room to do anything but fold against her. The walls of the space were stretchy and thin, but strong. She stretched her arm—her limb not quite following the instruction—like the message from her brain was

speaking a foreign language her body didn't understand. She wasn't in command of her own flesh. Not yet. It would take time, but she'd learn.

She was nearly ready to leave. Nearly strong enough.

A dull sound vibrated through the fluid cocoon. A familiar, comforting sound. Abruptly it increased in volume, until it nearly split her eardrums. The beat coming from outside doubled until it matched her heart's rhythm and she sloshed around as her cocoon jolted her this way and that. She didn't understand. Something wasn't right. Was it time to leave already?

Something hard and cold pierced the space, plunging deep into her leg and through her ribcage. Intense pain struck her heart, stopping it dead. Fluid drained from the cocoon as her body was drained of life.

No. I can't go; this isn't supposed to happen.

Her thoughts narrowed to a pinpoint. She reimagined the ending. Plugging up the hole and sucking it all back in, bringing herself back to life.

Shiloh felt a touch on her arm, her eyes springing open as she muffled her scream. The ceiling was inches from her face before her body crashed back to the bed, water drenching the sheets.

Zain was looking at his hand, apparently tracking a trickle of blood as it ran down his wrist. "I—"

The room spun as she sucked in a breath. Blood splatters covered his clothes. *What have I done? Oh, my God. What have I done?* "Zain! Are you okay?" She

reached for his hand, freezing at the sight of the bloodbath all over the bed. All over her. It was her blood, not Zain's. But the smell—Jax's smell—gripped her by the throat and squeezed.

"My hand passed right through yours. You weren't . . . solid." Zain's head wobbled on his neck, eyes widening as he reached for her.

What? How was that even possible?

Stumbling to the shower, she wrenched the faucet as far open as it could go, not caring that it was freezing cold. Red washed down her body. *Oh, my God. Oh, my God. Oh, my God. Is it time already?* That vision—she'd seen her death. But she'd been an innocent unborn baby. *God, it was so real.*

Chasing her shivers with a tentative touch, she couldn't find any obvious injury. There wasn't any pain. If anything, she felt invigorated. The water swirling down the drain started to clear, so the bleeding had stopped. If there had been any bleeding at all. She screwed up her nose. The blood carried the devil's scent, just like her own, but it was much stronger. If it wasn't impossible, she would've sworn it had been spilled by Jax's own veins.

Sliding her back down the tiles, she plonked on the floor under the chilled spray. She didn't want to know what had happened. She didn't want to go back to the bedroom. She couldn't face cleaning up another disaster.

Had that been a warning shot? A heads-up to prepare because death was on her heels, or the confirmation that she wouldn't even see it coming?

How much longer was death going to toy with her before it struck?

Shiloh almost wished it was over already. *If it wasn't for Lanie . . .*

Her head jerked up as a soaked ball of material flew past the shower, landing in the bath with a slap. Next came a couple of pillows.

"I'm coming in. If you're not decent, now's the time to say so." Zain waited through her silence for a solid minute before he entered, carrying the mattress.

He dumped it beside the bath, his cautious eyes finding hers. Reaching into the shower, he fiddled with the faucet, the water turning from icy to a warm embrace. "Are you in one piece?"

Shiloh dipped her chin in the affirmative.

His brow wrinkled as he looked her over before returning to the bath to rinse the bloody mess she'd made.

He was cleaning up after her.

She had no words.

Sitting up, she turned off the flow and crawled out to wrap herself in a towel.

He kept his back to her, diligently scrubbing at the sheets. "I don't know what the fuck is going on with you, but I think we'd better be safe and keep a distance

from now on. You'll have to sleep in the chair, or on the floor tonight. The video feed to your room is on a loop, but I'll have to flip it back in the morning. I can wrap the mattress in plastic to make the bed look normal for now. We'll figure out how to ditch it tomorrow." His voice trembled, almost stuttered.

She didn't reply. Her brain was still stuck on *keep a distance. Keep a distance. Keep a distance.*

She'd lost her biggest ally. Her only ally. And someone who could've possibly been a friend.

Fuck.

She welcomed the tears gathering in her eyes. Water always knew how to bring comfort, even if it meant purging her system was required. Crying was the one thing she *could* do.

"I'm sorry." Zain's shoulders curled in as he kept his back to her. "It's better this way. I won't mention this to anyone. They'll know I screwed around with the feed. But if you want to say something, I won't hold it against you. Do what ya gotta do. Maybe the doc should know about this." He hung his head for a beat before continuing to rinse the material.

He was right. It was better if she left him alone and just trusted Devlin to find her sister. How could she help anyone in the state she was in? Maybe that was why he'd shut her out. Maybe her body was breaking down faster than she knew. Didn't Lanie's kidnapping mean that Jax had already written Shiloh off and moved on to her younger sister? But the question of what he wanted with Lanie still remained unanswered.

The tiled walls closed in. She leant against the vanity, sliding back one cheek at a time until her butt was beside the basin and her spine was against the cold mirror.

"Just leave it, Zain."

"I got it."

"Forget it. I'll clean it up. There's clean sheets and towels in the closet. I've done this before. I can handle it."

"I don't think—"

"Get out."

His gaze collided with hers, his pupils huge. "Huh?"

"Leave." She choked on the word. "Please leave." *While you can.*

He dropped the sheets, wiping his hands on the back of his jeans as he hurried out.

Barely breathing, she let her head fall onto the mirror with a thunk. Her thoughts scattered until all that was left was a void. It was easier—less painful—to think of nothing.

Absolutely nothing.

Because if she acknowledged the reality of her position, she would shatter into a million pieces.

Chapter

Eleven

Sloppy

Margo combed her fingers through her blue hair, pushing it up so it spiked in all directions. "It's gotta be him. Twenty bodies pulled from the Hudson, all of them drained of blood, with their throats hanging by a thread? Come on, Sienna."

"Forensics are still at the scene. We don't know anything just yet. It's unlike him not to clean up his tracks."

"I ain't waitin'." Devlin crossed his arms, taking a seat on one of the desks in the control room. "We gotta check it out. Lock, Ren, I want you there. Take a team with you. Not the kid. I need him here riding the keyboards. Margo and Myles, you're with me. We ain't

leavin' Shiloh. Jax can't do nothin' with Lanie until her birthday. Until then, Shiloh is safe, but after that—" Devlin clawed the edge of the desk, splintering the wood. "After that, he's gonna be pissing blood from every orifice. Let me know what ya find. If it's him, hold him until I come. If he dies, she dies. That ain't gonna be good for the one with the loose trigger finger, so keep it tight. Go."

His team left the room, led by Sienna. Zain pushed his chair back like he was going to follow. "Zain."

The kid's head cranked around, his hand pausing its tug of war with the zipper of his hoodie. "Yeah?"

"I heard you got my girl safely to her room last night."

He made a choking sound before shifting his butt back in his seat. "Uh, yeah."

"I also heard you gone back to check on her this morning."

"The doc gave her some meds last night. I wanted to make sure she was okay."

"Is that right?" Devlin's face remained relaxed, but inside he was strung like a guitar. The kid was hiding something. He could feel vibrations coming off Zain's skull like he'd stowed a beehive in there. If Zain was playing him, Devlin wasn't gonna sing no melody. He'd snap and cut the little fucker. "And was she?"

"She was still sleeping. It was strong stuff." Zain tugged on the cord of his hoodie, his gaze meeting Devlin head on.

He cocked a brow. That wasn't what Myles had told him. Devlin's lip curled at the corner. It stung that the IT guy knew more about his girl than he did. What the fuck had the doc given her? *Damn it, I should have stayed with her.*

Why didn't I?

"Anythin' else you wanna tell me?"

A soft voice interrupted them. "Devlin."

His eyes shot to the doorway. The sight of Shiloh had his heart punching a few extra beats onto his ribcage.

"C-can we talk?"

He didn't like the lines on her forehead or the meekness of her voice. Nor the way her eyes sunk into dark pits above sharpened cheek bones. He fucking loathed the fear pulsing off of her. The way she gripped her right elbow while her right hand curled into a fist by her side. The way her shoulders reached for her earlobes. Her gaze colliding with Zain's before falling to Devlin's chest.

Nose twitching, he wrenched himself to his feet. *Jax.* She fucking reeked of him. "What the fuck?"

"It's not what you think."

"That ain't the sorta shit I wanna hear coming out of your mouth. Why is Jax's stench all over you?"

Her brows climbed. "Is it that bad?"

"Fuck yes, it is. What the fuck, Shiloh?" He gripped her by the shoulders, running his hands down her arms to reassure himself that she was still with him. "How—?"

"I don't know." Her eyes squeezed shut. When she opened them, it was Zain in her sights, not Devlin.

His head swiveled to the kid, vision blurred with smears of red.

Zain crossed his arms, tucking his hands into his armpits as he watched Shiloh. "I can tell you what I saw, but I can't explain it."

I'm gonna kill him.

Her hands crept under Devlin's shirt and around his waist, calm siphoning into his skin. "Promise me you'll hear him out. Don't hurt him."

He eased her to his side, facing Zain. "I ain't promisin' nothin'. Fucking tell me what happened before I lose my shit."

"I was dreaming. I think. Or—I dunno. I spaced out for a few minutes and it was like . . . like I was in my mother's womb. I heard our heartbeats and her voice. Then she started yelling and—" Shiloh's hand flew to her throat as she choked on the word. "She must've been stabbed. The blade went through my leg and into my chest. I died."

Fuck. She remembers.

Two hundred years ago in San Jose, she'd been taken from him. She'd had another name, another

body—but it was her soul, coming home to him. And she'd been taken before she was even born.

His throat clamped shut, his mind packing the memory back in its box and sealing that shit with ten rolls of duct tape.

Dragging in a breath, Shiloh continued. "That's when I woke up. I was nearly touching the ceiling." She snapped her mouth shut, darting a look at Zain.

"She was floating. But she wasn't—" He rubbed a hand across his forehead. "She was made of blood. Not flesh, or bone, not even hair. Just blood. She kinda just . . . splashed onto the bed."

"Splashed?" *Fuck me.* Hunger roared in Devlin's gut. He couldn't deny his craving for her blood. But, damn him, the fear of losing her stirred his stomach until the thought of feeding made it shrivel to the size of a walnut.

"Yeah, but then she was solid again. I told ya I couldn't explain it."

"Who the fuck was on the monitors last night?" He speared Zain with a look.

"I asked Zain to loop the feed," Shiloh interjected.

Heat blazed behind Devlin's eyes as he tried to lunge at Zain, but his body wouldn't obey his command. A growl rumbled from his lungs. Again, he tried, coming up against a barrier. Looking down at Shiloh, he saw flecks of color lighting up the caramel of her irises and an ethereal glow skimming under the surface of her skin.

She rested a hand on his chest, her eyes pleading as she shook her head.

She had power over him. And fuck him, it was turning him on. His arm tightened around her back. "Why?" What was she trying to hide?

"You think I like being on display? You can't keep me in a glass jar like a specimen to study. You won't tell me what's going on. You ordered me away. I *forced* Zain to help me."

The tension in Devlin's shoulders drained as he emptied his lungs in a rush. She was right. He thought he was protecting her, but he'd caged her. Taken away her rights.

The sparks in her eyes settled and her glow faded as she dropped her hand. He wobbled as the force holding his body eased off.

"I want to know more about Jax."

Devlin's nostrils flared. "Why can I smell him?"

"My best guess? We bonded. He was feeding me. My blood is his blood. That's the only thing I can think of."

Devlin ground his teeth and shook his head, denying her theory. "Nope. You smelled like you, not him. His scent faded after he ran."

Shiloh blinked, her hand reaching for her elbow again.

"He's right. You didn't smell like him before," Zain added.

Devlin cracked his neck, narrowing his eyes at the kid. Why was he still here? "Go play somewhere else."

The kid left so fast he sucked the air out of the room.

Shiloh turned in Devlin's arms. "That was rude."

"I don't give a fuck."

"You're going to turn them against you."

"They're vampires. I can't trust any of them."

Shiloh's shoulders tightened. "But I'm a vampire," she breathed.

Oh, babe. No, you're so much more.

Could he break his own vow and tell her the truth?

Could he trust her not to hate him if she knew?

————

Lanie awoke, jolting up onto her elbows, the sound of splintering wood crackling through the door. Something was on the other side trying to claw its way in. She twisted her head around, searching for anything she could use as a weapon as her spit dried to dust. All she had was a pillow. Her sheets. No lamp. Her water glass was gone.

Fuck.

The bedside table! She yanked out the top drawer, holding it on top of her still useless legs. A series of gunshots splintered the door in a deafening assault, the

decapitated handle rolling across the carpet. Lanie screamed as the door swung open. A ghostly white body hunched on the floor, gun in hand. His broad shoulders were bare, sporting skin so pale it was almost translucent. The bumps of each vertebra stood out, his torso heaving as he gasped for air. Letting go of the gun, he dug his fingers into the carpet, pulling his way along. Hair the color of ice hung over his face, masking his features. But she knew his shape.

"Seth?" She adjusted her grip on the drawer, her fingers trembling and slippery with sweat. What the fuck had happened to him? This wasn't the boy she knew. Whimpering, she tried in vain to get her legs to move. A mere twitch was the only feedback.

Her eyes darted back to his advancing form. He didn't speak. Or lift his head. As he got closer to the bed, she noticed the glint of a small knife in his other hand. *Fuck, fuck, fuck. Think!* Her feet continued to twitch as her heart rattled around in her ribcage. If she could knock him out, she'd have a chance to drag herself to safety. She threw the drawer down as hard as she could. It landed with a crack on his skull. His head dropped lower for a second before thrusting upwards. Two black pits in the place of eyes threatened to suck her in.

She screamed louder, her insides twisting in a massive knot. His hand latched onto her ankle, moving so fast she didn't see it coming. In the next breath she was in a heap on the floor. The slash of his knife bit at her wrist, blood pumping from the wound. He locked his mouth over her wrist, her essence draining into him. With her other hand, she pushed against his head. He was

too strong, even in his weakened state, not moving an inch. She fought heavy eyelids to stare as golden blond infused his hair with color, his skin slowly returning its tan. He pulled her wrist higher—sitting straighter—seeming to gain strength as she lost hers, her heartbeat reduced to a flutter. A core of ice spread its chill from deep within.

He dropped her wrist, a feral snarl coming from his lips. "I need more! Fucking succubus, she siphoned my blood. Your bitch sister is going to pay for this. As soon as she gives me what I want, she'll die just like his mother did. And I'll make him watch."

Lanie's eyes drifted shut. Splintering furniture sounded hollow in her ears before silence.

She wasn't sure if he was gone, or if she was checking out.

She had to hold on.

Shiloh. Help me.

Chapter

Twelve

Prophecy

Devlin rested his forehead on Shiloh's, gripping her a little closer.

"You—" It sounded like the words were strangling him. Puffing out his cheeks, he pulled back and looked her in the eye. "Babe . . ." Dragging the desk chair over, he urged her into the seat. "You and your sister, you ain't exactly average." Devlin shut his mouth, a crease forming between his brows as his dark gaze pulled her in. "My mam had a sister. She was with us the night they killed my mam. Magaidh saved me by hidin' me away. I knew she had a son who was older than me, but I never met him. His father took him from her when he was born. He had a wife who was barren, or

somethin' like that. But she was pregnant with another child when we left. I dunno who the kid's father was. Magaidh never married. A few days after we escaped, she died givin' birth. The kid didn't make it either.

"Years later, I searched for her older son. Turns out, he ended up in Spain working as a shipwright, married with a kid. You were the first female born into his lineage for more than five hundred years. The powers in your bloodline are dormant in males, but in females . . . you're a Lilin, babe. And so is Lanie."

The revelation plunged deep into her tissues finding every nook and cranny where her identity had burrowed, ripping it out by the roots.

"I—" She wanted to protest, but words escaped her. She blinked at his blurry form as he hovered in her line of sight. *How can it be true?*

"It ain't by sheer determination that you're the best swimmer in California."

Shiloh's eyes flared, heat flushing her body. *I worked my ass off to be the best.*

"You were popular, right? But ya didn't go to no parties. You was always studyin' or training. Come on, babe. You were popular 'cause people are drawn to you. Either that or your power threatens 'em. Lanie is workin' the threatening vibe like a champ." A smirk pulled on his lip. "But you ain't never had a chance to develop your true abilities because Jax fucked with your mind and took hold of your body. And now he wants to do the same to Lanie."

She shot to her feet. "No!"

"He can't turn her until she's sixteen."

"We only have three weeks until her birthday!"

"I know."

She paused, prickles skittering over her skin. What had Devlin said about his mother being a Lilin? "I thought this was about getting back at you. But he wanted me because I'm a Lilin, not because I'm your mate. That's why he wants Lanie."

"He took you away from me to stop me gaining full power and continuing my bloodline. But he also wanted something from you, and 'cause I took you back before he could get it, he went for your sister."

"What does he want?"

"He wants to rule his own race. And the way he thinks he'll do it is through creatin' his own bloodline of crossbreeds like me."

"He wants to . . . breed." Her whole body revolted at the thought—her uterus cramping as if it was throwing out a *hell no!* She heaved, the contents of her gut spewing all over the floor.

"Fuck!" He grabbed a trash can, shoving it under her face.

She bent forward, dry-retching, her body trying to purge his repugnant words from her mind. All the times she'd shared her body with Jax, the talk of eventually having a family one day—him, more enthused than she—it spilled out over the floor.

It didn't matter how many times she vomited, she'd never erase the fact that he'd been inside her.

Catching her breath, she swiped the back of her hand over her mouth and straightened up.

"You done?"

Shiloh nodded.

Devlin scooped her behind her knees and back, and raced up to his bathroom. Setting her on the side of the huge bath near the faucet, he turned on the water and aimed it over her legs to wash off the sick. She cupped her hands under the flow and rinsed out her mouth. He silently handed her a toothbrush and toothpaste.

He waited in silence as she finished cleaning up and dried off her legs. Wrapping herself in a towel to ward off the chill taking over her bones, she pinned him with a stare. "Is that possible? I thought you were a one-off."

Please say no.

"Truth? I ain't got a clue. Just 'cause some prophecy says I'm the first of a new race don't mean it's gonna happen. I always thought it was crap. Ain't no way I wanted to pull you into this fucking twilight zone bullshit."

"You didn't want to, but here I am. We can't ignore this. It's happening whether we like it or not. What did the prophecy say, exactly?"

"I can't remember the words she spoke. Somethin' about a retribution and salvation. We were hidin' in Dunfermline when she went into labor. My aunt

told me 'bout it just before she died. Said it was written in stone before I was born; I was the salvation. That I would right the wrongs, or some shit. Fuck! I can't remember. I was being hunted like an animal. My aunt was dying in my arms. I didn't give a fuck about some goddamn prophecy."

"I'm sorry. I know this must be hard, but it's important. Did she tell you where to find the prophecy?"

"No."

Shiloh's shoulders dropped. "Have you ever visited their graves?"

"No. I buried 'em near the abbey in Dunfermline. I ain't been back since." A shadow crossed his features.

Guilt tugged on her gut. He would have been a child, burying the only family he had left while he fought to survive. There'd be memories locked in his heart that he didn't want to free. She could see the pain simmering in his feverish eyes. She didn't want to be the one to use the key, but if he didn't face his pain, he was just as much a prisoner as those memories. She knew that as well as anyone. Trapped emotions were a festering wound that threatened to consume you from the inside out.

"After my shoulder healed, I followed Jax's trail to my mother's grave in Edinburgh. He left me a fucked up note but ran like a chickenshit before I could deliver my reply."

"Do you think he was looking for the prophecy?"

"My guess? He was leading me away from here so he could get to you. And I fell for it. I ain't left you since."

"You shut me out when Lanie went missing. You weren't with me when I started ch—" Her mouth snapped shut.

"When you started what?"

She rubbed her forehead, forcing a breath out of her nose. "Something is happening to me. You saw what I did to Ren. You heard what happened in my room. I'm changing."

"You're finding your power. Lilith's power."

"What do you know about Lilith?"

"She was Adam's first wife."

"Adam? As in Adam and Eve, Adam?"

"Yeah. In the Bible, the Book of Genesis says that God created male and female at the same time. But then later on, a woman was created from his rib 'cause he was moaning about not having a suitable companion. The first female was Lilith."

"What happened to her?"

"She didn't kneel to Adam's macho bullshit. She grew wings and flew the fuck out of the garden, refusing to come back. She was cursed for it. After she hooked up with pops, hundreds of her children died for her sins."

"So she's not a demon?"

"Adam probably thought she was."

"How did your mother and aunt survive?"

"Just lucky, I guess."

"I don't think so. I think it has something to do with the prophecy. Your mom was meant to bring you into the world and your aunt was meant to get you to safety. I think they knew they had to sacrifice themselves." Shiloh's gaze dropped to her feet. *Just like me.* She lifted her chin, that one movement requiring more strength than she thought possible. "What happened to your dad?"

"Magaidh got me outta there before they busted down the door. I heard him yelling and my mam's screams as we ran. We saw the smoke rising from the fire for miles."

Shiloh didn't say a word. She couldn't form anything worthy of releasing from her tongue.

"After Magaidh and the baby died, I risked going home. I had to know what happened. I found her charred remains a half a mile from the cabin. There were more bodies in the cabin, maybe one of them was my da. But hers was in the field at the base of a wooden pole. I knew it was her, 'cause I found a necklace she used to wear a few feet away. They were prepped for a witch hunt. I had to bury her. I couldn't leave her there. She didn't get the headstone she deserved until years later. I made sure of it before I came to America."

"You did the right thing."

He closed his mouth, crossing his arms.

Shiloh sucked in her bottom lip, thinking back to her dream and all the blood she'd shed. "But what was my dream about? And why was I covered in Jax's blood?"

Flames engulfed Devlin's pupils. "I'd like to know why the fuck his blood was all over you, too." D curled his hands into fists, the sound of bones crunching sending shivers down her spine.

"When I woke up, my head was a mess, but my body . . . felt like I'd just had a binge after starving for so long. Is it possible that he gave me his blood somehow?"

"I—fuck." He cracked his neck, grinding his teeth. "If I think about his blood in you I'mma destroy somethin'."

He paced across the room, his footfalls heavy enough to break some tiles. Picking up a shard, he ran the tip of his finger over the sharp point, drawing a drop of blood. Shiloh's throat closed, her hand curling into the towel as she watched him suck it into his mouth.

Blinking rapidly in an attempt to clear her scarlet vision, she backed towards the door in case she needed to run. She couldn't give in to the pull. As much as she wanted to gorge on him, it was a pleasure she'd always be denied. He threw the shard into the sink, snapping her out of her thoughts.

"The dream you had, it wasn't a dream. It was a memory." The light behind Devlin's eyes snuffed out.

Her lips parted with the breath leaving her lungs. *It's true. The dream was so real.* "I—I think I believe you."

"You were supposed to come to me two hundred years ago. Your parents lived in San Jose. Your mother was close to giving birth. I was keeping watch. Margo was with me." Gripping the edge of the bench, he dropped his head. "He stabbed your mom in the stomach. We didn't see him coming."

"Him?"

"Jax."

"Jax!? But he only went missing two years ago."

Devlin rubbed a hand over his stubble, lines collecting at the corners of his eyes. "I killed him after he murdered you and your mom. I thought that was the end of it. That the prophecy was broken or somethin'. But you came back . . . and so did he."

"Goddamn it, Devlin. What else haven't you told me? If we're going to save my sister and end this, we've gotta work as a team. You say you can't trust anyone—why can't you trust me? My sister's life is on the line. I have way more to lose than you. If you keep blocking me, I will find a way past. You can't control this."

"I can't lose you again."

"I am dying. Either way, I'm dying. Don't let it be in vain."

Devlin's expression crumbled, the construction of bravado toppling. He spun away, hiding his face. His shoulders seemed to bend under some great weight. A force yanked on her heart, pulling her into him. Damn, he was fighting this so hard. These moments of vulnerability were the cracks in his porcelain. They

weren't flaws, but marks of character that made him infinitely more beautiful to her. He hadn't been pushing her away to hurt her. It was his way of padding up to reduce the impact when the inevitable blow landed.

Dropping the towel, Shiloh crossed the space between them and enfolded him in her arms. She rested the side of her face on his warm back. "Don't shut me out."

His chest expanded, pushing against her cheek before shuddering under her embrace.

Rough palms covered her hands, that one touch telling her more than she ever needed to know.

"I'm still here. We have now. Can't we take what we've got?" Tugging on one of her arms, he pulled her around in front of him. His huge form engulfed her, strong arms lifting her off her feet so their lips could meet. She wrapped her legs around his waist, anchoring herself. Anchoring him. Cupping her butt, he walked them to the vanity and sat her on the benchtop. His arms stayed coiled around her. His face burrowed into her neck, telling her he never wanted to let her go. If she had a choice, she'd never let him. But that was fantasy. All they had was now. It was all anyone ever had. Everything else was just memories and dreams.

His fingertips slipped under the waistband of her shorts, sending tingles over her skin. One hand crept lower while the other retreated upwards, taking the edge of her shirt with it.

"I need skin." The words were raked out over hot coals.

She indulged him, slipping off her tee. He pulled back. His bloodshot eyes roamed her body. Reaching behind his neck, he dragged his shirt over his head and dumped it on top of hers.

Oh. My. God.

Heat bloomed in her core like he'd lit her on fire. She pursed her lips, blowing out a long, slow breath. Control. She had to keep control. "How far can this go before we're in danger?"

Please. I need . . . She squeezed her thighs together. Her desire threatened to singe her from the inside out.

"I can't have you how I want you. But I can damn sure give you somethin' to remember."

They reached for each other at the same time— him burying his face in her cleavage, her fingers diving into his hair. Her bra disappeared in one skillful movement before his mouth latched onto her nipple. He lapped at her breast, his fangs guiding it home through the goal posts. And, damn, she'd scored big having him all to herself.

She ran her hands over his shoulders feeling his power coil, ready to strike. She trusted him not to unleash it. Having his fangs bracketing her sensitive nipple had her salivating at the thought of them plunging in and drinking their fill. Her fangs lengthened, ready to follow through on that fantasy. Swallowing, Shiloh threw her head back, gasping for air. She had to make sure she kept herself on lockdown, too. He was just as much at risk as she was. *We still have this.* Their bond was deeper

than any artificially induced imitation. They'd been several lifetimes in the making. This was fate. That could never be broken.

His mouth didn't stop as his hands slid down to the zipper of her shorts. He tugged until she leaned back on her hands. Lifting her ass, he stripped her bare. The cold, hard stone surface was a stark contrast to her soft heat, sending a shock up her spine. His fingers played along the newly exposed flesh, squeezing and caressing.

Worshipping.

He was worshipping his queen.

One finger dipped into the hollow at her throat and slowly drew a line down between her breasts, his tongue doing a chaser, straight down the middle to her hot center. She cried out as he made contact, sucking, licking, working her with his fingers. Her hands yanked at his hair, her gasps amplified and bouncing off the tiled walls. Her world tilted, and a split second later, he had her on his mattress, his shoulders pushing her thighs wide open. He was in complete command, and for once in her life, she was ready to surrender all control.

Her pleasure built, hands clawing at the sheets until a wave of exquisite sensation crested. And crested. Her body quaked uncontrollably.

She didn't want it to stop.

She begged for it to stop.

I can't take it anymore.

I want more.

Her legs scissored, pushing him away. He raised his head, licking his lips. His gaze flickered with blue and green sparks. He dipped his head again, kissing the insides of her thighs.

She lay spent, her heart fuller than it had ever been, and wanting to give him the loving he deserved in return. "What about you?"

"No, babe. It's all about you tonight."

Oh. My.

"I fucking hate that I can't give you what you deserve. You should have big-ass bunches of flowers and dirty weekends away in five-star hotel rooms. I want you sleeping with me every night."

Sounds like heaven to me. She brushed his hair away from his face, giving him a cheeky grin. "We can have a date night in. Wanna go eat ice cream and chill in front of a film? Or, you know, do bad things that would normally get us kicked out of the movies." She licked her lips as her mind started wandering to all sorts of possibilities.

He coughed out a laugh. "Yeah."

They didn't leave the room all night.

Chapter

Thirteen

Wait Up, What?

Shiloh took a seat next to Margo at the kitchen table.
Through the windows, pink and orange streaked across
the horizon as the encroaching night dimmed the blue
sky. Coffee and cinnamon scented the stale air. Shiloh
hooked a finger in the neck of her T-shirt and gave it a
couple of tugs. How long had it been since she'd been
outside?

"Any word from New York?" *Please tell me they
didn't drag Lanie from the Hudson.* "D-did they find my
sister?"

"She wasn't there, honey." Margo patted Shiloh's
hand before reaching for her coffee.

Shiloh's shoulders dropped. *Thank God.* She wanted to find her sister, but not floating face-down in a filthy river.

Where the hell are you, Lanie?

"But we're pretty sure Jax was and now we finally have a place to search."

It wasn't much, but it was more than they'd had in a long time.

Hold on, Lanie. Please hold on.

Margo took a sip before continuing. "Ren commented that he's getting sloppy. Something must have happened to cause him to have a blood orgy. The NYPD pulled seven bodies. Our insider said none of them were vamps. Whoever killed them didn't intend on turning them."

"How do you know? Maybe the killer was scared off."

"True, I guess. But seven?" Margo's brow bunched. "That's a lot of digging. And once they're reborn, their sire has to feed them all."

Shiloh clasped her hands together. "What if it was more than one vampire?"

Margo shook her head. "Lock reckons it was definitely a single vampire. The bodies have been taken for autopsy. The wounds were almost all identical. The poor bastards were probably sightseeing and got more than they bargained for. He must've had help rounding up his prey."

Shiloh tilted her head. "But why would he drink human blood if he had vampires available?"

"Maybe they were bonded. He would've needed help keeping seven humans immobilized for long enough to drain them. Vampire persuasion only works to a point. If a human senses mortal danger, all bets are off. There were no signs of a blow to the head, or abrasions from restraints. If he was in full bloodlust, he wouldn't have had the patience to tie them up or knock them out, anyway. This has Jax written all over it."

Shiloh spread her fingers on the table top, watching them as her thoughts churned. "What if he'd been starving, like someone had drained him too much? Would that cause him to have to drink so many to death?"

"Sounds legit. But he's too smart to let anyone do that to him."

What if she didn't need to get close? What if her connection with him was enough that she could tap into it somehow and drain him? And if she could hurt him . . . could he hurt her too?

There was no way she could tell Margo what happened the night before. Not after Zain's reaction. She hadn't seen him since they'd come clean to Devlin. "Yeah. He *was* too smart before. But if he's behind the slaughter of these people, he's slipping. I want to go to New York."

"Not a chance."

"Lanie's there somewhere."

"We don't know that."

"If I get close, I'll be able to feel him."

"Honey, there is no way in hell Devlin, or any of us, for that matter, will let you within spitting distance of that son of a bitch."

"I'm Lanie's greatest hope. You're risking her life to save mine when mine's already over. It's the stupidest . . . shit!" She pressed her fists into the sides of her head. "We have to play smart. Let's remove the emotion and use our brains. Jax *knows* I can find him. He also knows you won't risk me that way. So why don't we do what he's not expecting? I'm still here, so the bond isn't broken. I want to be the one to break it."

Margo whistled and shook her head. "If it was up to me, that speech would've had me buying you a plane ticket to the big apple, but honey, D won't do it. Not ever."

This is just fucked.

Letting her head flop back, Shiloh eyed the ceiling. What was it gonna take? They were letting Jax have all the power.

"I'm going for a swim." The chair legs scraped on the floor as she stood.

"You sure you've got the energy?" Margo raised her brows, the hint of a smirk on her lips.

"I'm fine."

"I bet you are. Anything else you want to share?"

Shiloh's face flushed with heat.

"No words necessary, honey. That face says it all."

She trapped a few curse words on her tongue as her eyes narrowed. Typical Margo. She was so blasé about the important things. Life. Death. Love. It was all a fucking joke, apparently.

"You know what, Margo? It's none of your fucking business." Shiloh headed for the door.

"Oh, come on! Devlin's rubbing off on you." She burst out laughing. "For real, I swear I didn't plan that joke. But it was perfect."

Fuck off. The woman did not know when to stop.

Passing through the exit, she saw movement at the far end of the hallway. *Dark hair. That's Sienna.* She disappeared into the clinic. Shiloh followed, sticking her back to the wall beside the door. *I'll wait all damn night for her if I have to.* Sienna had inside knowledge on the situation in New York. Shiloh wanted to pick her brain.

". . . doesn't know."

"She's unaware. I'm sure of it."

Oh, shit, the door's open a crack. I'd better give them some privacy. Shiloh peeled her back off the wall and took two steps.

"Good. Have we done another blood test since the incident?"

Incident? Shiloh froze before she about-faced.

"No. I won't need another sample until twenty-weeks' gestation."

Um . . . gestation?

"I'd like another test *now*. I have a theory I'm trying to dispel."

"Certainly. I'll go by her room in the morning."

"She'll be in the east wing. He wants her with him for her last days."

Holy fuck, they're talking about me! Gestation? Are they talking about pregnancy? Last days?

"Don't wait up for me tonight. I'll be back in the morning. Keep me updated."

"Of course."

Shiloh scurried into the theatre room, gluing one eye to a tiny gap in the door. She counted to three. *Sienna didn't pass. Why didn't she pass?*

Opening the door wider, Shiloh risked a peek, catching sight of Carter vanishing under the staircase.

Was there a basement? A secret exit? *Of course there frickin' is.* If they were under attack, they'd need a way to get out safely.

Shiloh backed up and closed the door, gliding to one of the chairs in a daze. Her palms covered her belly. Was there a baby growing in there? Her baby?

Jax's baby.

Her stomach rolled.

Torn between amazement and disgust, she stared at her stomach feeling a whole new level of empathy for Sigourney Weaver's character in *Alien*. He'd planted his

spawn. Was the baby the reason for her new abilities? If she was gaining power, was Jax able to tap into that, too? He'd gotten just what he wanted. He'd successfully stolen Devlin's birthright . . .

And he wouldn't need Lanie anymore.

Oh, my God.. If he finds out, he's going to kill her!

Shooting to her feet, Shiloh hustled to the door and flung it open. *Shit! The cameras.* Feigning composure, she walked up to her room and into the closet. She threw some clothes and supplies in her backpack and got into her warmest outfit. That scarf from her mom was going to come in handy after all. *Mom, Dad, I hope you're okay. I'm going to bring her home.* She'd have to bolt at full speed if she had any hope of avoiding the cameras. But it didn't matter if they came after her, as long as she had a head start.

Securing the pack in place, she closed her eyes and blew out a breath. She hadn't had a chance to test her powers, but she had a feeling—

If Devlin is right . . . if I really am a Lilin . . . I hope this works.

Light as a feather. I'm as light as a feather.

She wobbled, throwing out her arms for balance as her shoes rose a foot off the ground.

Yes! Fuck. I hope this works.

She streaked out. A split second later, she faced the spot where she'd watched Sienna disappear. There was no door. How the hell? Giving the wall a shove, she was met with solid resistance. *No, no, no!*

Shiloh balled her hands into fists. Scarlet bled across her vision. A high-pitched ringing almost deafened her as energy pulsed from deep within. Heavy footfalls on the stairs vibrated from above. *Fuck.* She raised her hands and imagined the wall disintegrating as she shoved again, backing the action with all her power. The wall crumbled to dust, exposing what was left of a doorframe leading down another level. Choking on the concrete dust, she jumped, taking ten steps at a time.

"Shiloh!" Devlin's deep voice threatened to bowl her down.

She raced down a long hallway, green metal doors flashing by in a blur. Another metal door blocked her escape at the end. Heaving her power, she blew the barrier off its hinges, the sound mimicking a car crash. The twisted steel remains tumbled for a few feet before falling over the edge of a cliff.

"Stop, Shiloh!"

I'm sorry. I love you.

She jumped through the gaping hole and followed the door over the edge.

"Noooooo!" His roar echoed through the valley below.

Her legs kicked, her arms pinwheeling. Cold air rushed under her jacket. Her backpack pushed up under her ponytail. Her heart threatened to bail out.

Light as a feather. Light as a feather.

Fuuuuuck! Pain ripped through her shoulder blades as black, blood-drenched wings tore from her

flesh. Her backpack and jacket were flung off completely, the items plummeting towards the ground. Her body abruptly shunted upwards, knocking the breath from her lungs. She flexed her new appendages, rising higher.

Holy fucking shit! Lanie is going to love this.

She spun around, spotting Devlin standing at the edge of the cliff, watching her. The guards gathered in the yard, mouths agape. Margo waved from the patio, grinning as she raised her mug of coffee. Zain stood at the windows, headphones in his hand, jaw on the floor.

Thank you for keeping me safe, but I have to do this.

She started to turn away, but caught sight of Devlin, taking off his jacket and shirt. Two massive obsidian wings unfurled from his back. He speared her with a look, his eyes licked with flames.

Oh. My. God. Check him out.

Her core clenched. It was so wrong to be turned on, but faced with her avenging angel in all his glory, she had no choice. They were equals in every way. This was why the Fates had put them together.

Her mouth curled in a seductive smile. Flapping her wings, she mouthed an invitation before speeding off.

Come and get me.

Chapter

Fourteen

If Only the Trees Could Talk

Tumbling in a ball of feathers and skin, Shiloh and Devlin crashed into the wilderness somewhere in New York State. Her lungs burned, surging in a bid for more air. White-hot pokers stabbed into her shoulder blades. She hissed as she dug out a rock from under her hip before rubbing the bruise it had left behind.

In the moonlight, the bare oak trees looked like ghostly skeletons, guarding their territory. An eerie calm cloaked the mysteries stored in their wood and sent Shiloh's senses pricking.

Death has been here.

Shivering, she shook out her feathers and cocooned herself inside her wings. Wearing only jeans and a bra, she was in danger of freezing to death in the November night air. She'd lost the rest of her T-shirt somewhere over Kansas and she had no idea what had happened to the scarf.

Devlin jumped to his feet, his body overshadowing her huddled form. "What the fuck were you thinking?"

"It's-s the . . ." She gasped for air between words. ". . . on-ly w-way."

"We can't stay here."

"He's n-near." The sickening tug of the membrane had pulled her from the sky. "I f-feel it."

"Exactly why we gotta get the fuck away." He scooped her up and took off.

Below them, the sparse scattering of houses looked like tiny boxes, dim light spilling from their windows. As they got closer to town, the gaps between neighbors narrowed. He landed on the roof of a shop, tucking his wings out of sight as he put her back on her feet.

"Put your wings away. We don't wanna get caught on camera."

Goosebumps traced the withdrawal of his embrace as she wondered how the hell she was going to do that. "I don't know how."

"Imagine them going back in and they will."

She gave it her best shot. It took a few seconds for her wings to respond, but she did it. Jiggling her shoulders, she adjusted to the weight she now carried. It was uncomfortable, but nowhere near as painful as setting them free.

"You'll get used to it. It won't hurt as bad the next time you whip 'em out."

She wrapped her arms around her waist, trying to stop her shivers. "Why did you bring us here?"

"I ain't lettin' you walk around half-naked. And we need to chill for a bit until I round up the team."

"I don't think the shops are open."

"The liquor store is."

"They don't sell clothes."

"Who said anything 'bout buyin' clothes?"

He grabbed her hand and tugged her to the edge of the roof. They crouched down, staying hidden in the shadows as they surveyed the scene across the street.

Central Park, Liquors. Peekskill, New York. The store logo used Old English font and featured two winged lions protecting two bottles of wine topped by a crown.

Two winged predators.

Red wine—symbolizing blood—topped with a crown.

Royal blood.

How appropriate.

Devlin pointed to the street. "See that guy over there? Bushy beard. Leather jacket."

Bushy Beard was heading into the bright lights of the lion's den. "Yeah."

"I reckon he's 'bout my size. And he's got a girl waitin' in the truck."

Shiloh gave him a sidelong glance. "What are you going to do?" She didn't like the gleam in his eye.

"The truck is heated. They'll live."

"Devlin."

"Do you wanna die of frostbite before we get Lanie back?"

Good point. "No."

He raised his eyebrows and turned his attention back to the store. Loaded up with two bottles of something and a six-pack of beer, the guy exited the store.

"Wait here." Leaping to the ground, Devlin reached into his jean pocket, pulling out a smoke as he strolled across the street.

"Hey, man. Got a light?"

The guy's head snapped around to face Devlin, his shoulders pulling in to his ears. He stood still for a whole minute, watching D hold up his smoke. "No. Sorry."

"Damn shame. That's a nice jacket. You wanna give it to me, don'tcha?"

The guy bent to put his drinks on the sidewalk before shucking off the leather. He handed it over, no questions.

His girl opened the door of the truck, but Devlin pointed a finger in her direction, shutting her in.

If she sensed any danger, this could go to shit.

"I'd like to meet your woman."

Bushy Beard started to lead the way.

"What about your alcohol?" Devlin picked up one of the bottles, inspecting the label.

The guy spun back, grabbing the remaining stash. He held out a palm for D's bottle.

"Not this one. You don't really want it."

The beard shook his head and carried on his way.

Reaching the truck, Devlin opened the door for his new friend. "Hi, I'm Dean. Your man is somethin' else, helping me out on a cold night. Thanks for your help. What did ya say your names were, again?

"Jack. And this is Erin."

"Erin. I like it. You're too hot wearing that in here. Take it off. I'll look after it, I swear."

Shiloh couldn't see the woman's face, and if she spoke at all, she was super-quiet. But two minutes later, Devlin was knocking on the roof of the truck and walking away with a bottle of whiskey, a leather jacket, his and hers matching Henleys, and a hooded women's puffer jacket.

Shiloh felt slightly sick. It wasn't that she was ungrateful for his skills. She just knew what it was like to be on the wrong end of vampire manipulation. If she could repay those people for their gifts, she would somehow.

Dev leaped up to where she was hiding. "I know you don't like it, but it's what we gotta do to survive." He put the bottle of Jack down and handed over the clothes.

"I know."

After throwing on his new Henley, he reached both arms into the leather. "I called Lock. They're on their way. I gotta get a few more things. Get dressed." Adjusting the jacket collar, he took the Jack and jumped to the ground. "Meet me inside."

She wrestled the clothes over her trembling body and followed him inside the neighboring convenience store.

Devlin rested one elbow on the counter. "Babe. Good news. The Doritos and Coke are free for tonight. Ain't that amazin'?"

She nodded, watching the store clerk pack the crisps and cola into a bag.

"Throw in some jerky and a lighter while you're at it."

The guy did as he was told.

Shiloh clamped her mouth shut before she yelled, *stop!* Deciding it was better to wait outside, she left them to it. The bond tugged her down the street in the direction

they'd come. She stumbled a couple of steps before planting her feet. Jax knew she was near. There was no way he wasn't feeling the same pull.

Was he going to come after her?

No. He's guarding Lanie. If she's alive.

Shiloh was going to have to go and get him.

Could he sense his flesh forming life inside her?

She couldn't feel anything. She hadn't seen the blood results. What proof did she have? *None*. Her eyes strayed back to the convenience store as Devlin came out. Maybe she should ask for a pregnancy test.

He stopped in front of her, his brows dropping low. "What's wrong?"

Looking at his haul of stuff, she realized something. *He's stalling. He's never going to surrender to what has to happen. He knows.* "Am I pregnant?"

The bag rustled as he switched his grip. "Yes."

"How long have you known?"

"I knew the moment it happened."

Her eyelids suddenly felt heavier than her newly acquired wings.

"If this was a conventional relationship, you'd be out on your ass. You've repeatedly hidden things from me. I know you said you've never lied to me, but in my book that's as good as lying." She shivered, crossing her arms. "You've kept me locked up. You've prevented me from doing right by my sister. I know you didn't choose this. I know you've done everything to protect me.

Maybe I'm not being fair, but you haven't been fair, either." Her brows pulled together in anguish. "I need to do this on my own. He's won. Game over. You know death isn't the end. I've come back before. I've loved you for hundreds of years." She met his black gaze. "We'll find each other again. I've got to go. You need to let me go now."

"I can't."

"You don't have a choice."

She bolted, not looking back. If he wanted to catch her, he could. He didn't. *Good.* She swiped at her tears, waiting until she was out of town before taking off her shirt and jacket. After balling them up, she set her wings free and took flight, letting the membrane carry her to her end.

She didn't have to go far.

Landing in the woods of Bear Mountain, she tucked her wings away and got dressed. Through the trees she could see smoke curling from a chimney. Jax's scent lingered on the breeze.

And so did Lanie's. It was almost overpowering.

Like he'd spilled her blood. *Fuck!*

Shiloh ran at the cabin. Aiming a rope of power at the door, she clawed her hand and ripped it off its mooring. Vampires swarmed at her, trailing from the doorway like ants leaving their nest. More dropped down from the barren branches of the trees. Her sight was nearly eclipsed by the onslaught. Pulling in all her energy, she rained hellfire onto the masses.

"Shiloh!"

Flanking her, Lock, Ren, and Devlin had weapons of their own. Ren slashed at the advancing vampires with twelve-inch daggers. Lock pumped off rounds from a pair of Glocks, a shotgun strapped to his back ready to go. Devlin burned them to a crisp with his own brand of hellfire and crushed them to a pulp with the twist of his hand.

Jax's army kept coming. Fangs ripped into flesh. Fists crushed. Bones snapped. The sound of combat howled like a storm. The cloak of calm was totally obliterated as the trees spilled their secrets, soaking up the blood of their guests.

Shiloh's power was draining. She kept a barrier of energy around her, but it was getting weak. Sensing Jax nearby, she wondered why he hadn't engaged. He was probably perched in a tree with a box of popcorn. *Fucker*.

The ground shook as something fell from the sky. Twisted together in a ball of rage, Jax was locked in a fist fight with something huge. Something with fangs. The male landed a punch to Jax's chest, sending him flying into a tree. He flopped to the ground with a thud. Standing to his full height, the stranger rivalled Devlin and Lock in the size department. Cropped black hair framed a face carved from clay akin to Devlin's. And he was shirtless. Like Devlin. A massive tattoo depicting a pair of wings covered both sides of his chest. Who was he?

The vampire drew a sword from a holster at his back, chasing after his prey.

"Stop!" Devlin roared, running after him. "You'll kill her, too."

The sky spun upside down as she was knocked on her ass. Shaking the fog from her head, she found Ren standing over her, slashing at Shiloh's attacker. Christ, the vampire had no face left. Shiloh yanked her eyes away, but it was too late. She'd never forget the sight. It would probably follow her into the afterlife.

"Get up and fucking pay attention," Ren barked.

Shiloh stumbled to her feet, rebuilding the bubble of energy she used to fend off intruders. "Thanks."

"Don't mention it. Ever."

God, she couldn't deal with Ren's snarky shit right now. Where the hell was Lanie? Shiloh needed to get inside to find her sister. She remembered Devlin's Moses act from the first night at Fluid Prey. What the hell? Whatever he could do, she could do, too. She pressed her palms together, extended her arms, and scooped the air in front like she was doing breaststroke. Just like the night at the club, bodies stacked up in walls, clearing a path to the entrance. She ran through, letting them all collapse behind her.

Christ, the smell of rancid blood and urine nearly knocked her down. She went straight for the bedrooms. Only one of them had a lock on the outside. She pointed at it, busting it open. *Oh, my God.* Lanie's body lay in a heap on the crusty carpet. A huge brown stain bloomed around her. How long had she been there like that? The sheet had been pulled from the bed and ripped. Strips of the torn sheets were bandaged around her wrist, their

color matching the stain on the carpet. Had Lanie slit her wrist? Or was it Jax?

"Get her out of here!"

Devlin stood at Shiloh's back, fending off vampires as they rushed in. Lock's gun made Swiss cheese of the enemy and splintered the walls from somewhere within the cabin. They were covering her. *Evren must still be outside on her own. Shit.*

Shiloh looked at the window. It wasn't a clear exit. They were surrounded.

How do I get her out?

Her head snapped up. Of course. She yanked off her top and covered Lanie as best as she could before releasing her wings. Gathering her sister's body in her arms, she aimed a fist at the ceiling. She only managed to make a crack in the plaster. Devlin backed into the room, his wings already spread. He hooked his arm around her and blew a hole in the ceiling. Thrusting up with powerful legs, he got them airborne, setting them down in a field a few miles away.

"Is she alive?"

Lanie's pulse fluttered against Shiloh's fingers. "Yes."

"Can you fly?"

"I think so."

"Head to Greenwich. We have a safe house in Milbank Avenue. Number two fifty-three." He pressed a

phone into her hand. "Call the contact named Med. They'll help her."

She nodded, and took off, not knowing where the hell to go. Greenwich was towards the southeast. She'd get close and use the GPS to find her way from there. "Please hold on, Lanie."

Déjà-frickin'-vu.

Hadn't they done this before? She was abandoning him in a fight to try and save her sister's life yet again. This time he had his team with him. And they wouldn't stop until they had Jax.

Jesus H. Christ. When would this end?

Chapter

Fifteen

Don't be Daft

Devlin scanned the trees for his target. The fallen corpses bled streams of blood in a crimson delta. Ren plucked through the carnage, stabbing into lifeless bodies. *Nobody gets away with playing dead.* Lock plucked off a couple more escapees before dragging their bodies onto the pile.

Where is he? Devlin spotted the glint of a sword in the spot where he'd left Shiloh and Lanie. Guided by the beacon, he rocketed to the ground, sending up a spray of rocks and dirt.

The stranger's legs were braced wide, his chest tat splattered with blood, dirt, and sweat. The vampire's palm was wrapped tightly around the hilt of his sword,

blanching his knuckles as his midnight gaze stared Devlin down. The leather strap of his sword harness lay at his feet.

Devlin stalked towards the vampire. "Who the fuck are you?"

"That's a daft question, brother." His tongue curled the R's into a Scottish brogue.

You ain't no brother of mine, Scot.

The intruder threw the sword down as a huge pair of wings sprouted from his back. His feathers shuddered, capturing the moonlight and extinguishing its glow in their darkness.

"Half brother, to be exact. I've been searching for ye for centuries."

Half brother? The guy had wings. They weren't from dear old dad. And his mother hadn't had any other children. That he knew of.

"I saw your handiwork on yer mam's grave. I put it to rights."

So they didn't share a mother. Who else had his father fucked over? "Who's your mam?"

"Isn't it obvious?" He flexed his wings. "Magaidh is my mam. You helped her birth me. I survived."

"I buried you."

"That you did. And she dug me out, with the help of a friend."

"She's alive?"

"Not in the least." He crossed his arms. "But the absence of a body doesn't denote the absence of spirit, brother. Energy cannot be destroyed. Our mothers walk beside us, always."

Devlin pressed the pads of his thumbs into his eye sockets. If that was true, they'd never destroy Jax. "How'd he escape?"

"Two of them carried him away while I slaughtered another ten. He had the numbers on his side. But now that he doesn't have blood protection, he'll do poorly trying to recruit more troops. And I gave him a fairly sizable gash on his thigh. They'll tend to him all right, but he'll take a while to recover without her blood."

"Blood protection. That's how he's managed to ghost me."

"Lilin blood. The blood of our ancestors. The scent was all over him. Those poor girls must've been his pin cushions."

Fuck me.

Devlin lit up a smoke, his mind wandering to the sisters. *I hope they made it.*

The vampire picked up his harness. "Did the girl survive?"

"Lanie?"

"Lanie. So that's her name." The guy's tongue licked at the word like he was starving for a taste, his eyes sparking with colors.

"Fuck, no. Leave her the fuck alone."

"Like you left her sister? That worked out for the best, now, didn't it?"

Asshole.

———

Two fifty-three Milbank Avenue was not a house. It was a bunker. The way in was through the sewer. Shiloh had landed and huddled with Lanie under a tree in the small park before dialing the contact.

Now she found herself waiting in a moldy staff room while the medical team tried to stabilize her sister. Lanie needed blood. A lot of blood. How she'd stayed alive, Shiloh had no clue. How much more could one person endure?

The door swung open and Lock and Ren walked in. The pair of them were soaked with sweat, and filthy from head to toe.

"Hey." Lock tipped his chin.

"She alive?" Ren inspected her fingernails, boredom painting her expression.

Shiloh dropped her head in her hands, her heart dropping in her chest. "I don't know."

"They'd have told you if she'd punched her card." Evren went to the sink and washed her hands, splashing water on her face. "I'll go check it out."

Shiloh closed her eyes, hearing the fridge open and shut, and the sound of gulping, followed by a

satisfied sigh. A pair of boots stepped into view. She lifted her eyes. "Thirsty?" Lock offered her a bottle of water

Shaking her head, she let it fall forward again.

"She's not gonna die."

"How do you know?"

"I don't."

Very comforting. Thanks, Lock.

"I didn't like you at first, but I see it now. You and D, you're a good fit."

His opinion should've made her feel better, but it stung. Her and Devlin's 'fit' was meant to break. Jax had to die and he'd take Shiloh with him.

The door opened again and in walked Devlin, and the vampire from the cabin. Lock lurched to his feet, putting the barrel of his gun in the stranger's face. Devlin shook his head, and Lock holstered his weapon.

"This is Rory." D hooked his thumb in the guy's direction.

Black eyes took her in, and she stood. Rory's gaze reached inside her, connecting to something. A piece from her past? Another life?

"My brother," Devlin added.

"Fuck me," Lock uttered, staring at the guy, still holding his bottle.

Rory gave Shiloh a bow in greeting. Her lips parted. With the two of them side by side, it was obvious.

Same body, same nose, eyes and cheek bones. His mouth wasn't as hard. His hair was much shorter. He didn't radiate anger like Devlin did. But they were siblings, for sure.

Was he a crossbreed too? She'd seen his fangs, but no wings—apart from the tattooed variety.

What did that mean for the prophecy?

"Your brother." Her brows pulled together. "How—?"

"Half brother." Rory interjected.

He's Scottish. Did they share a mother, or father? Why was he here? Had he been tracking Jax too?

She stacked her queries as he continued. "Although, I personally believe a brother is a brother whether they're full, half, adopted, or a ring-in. It's a position of honor."

Dev turned to her. "Do you remember me telling you about the child Magaidh lost during labor?"

She nodded.

"He lived. This is Magaidh's son. We share a father."

So he *was* a crossbreed. Had Magaidh had an affair with her sister's husband, or had she been forced? Maybe she'd loved him. They'd never know.

"I've been waiting to meet Devlin my whole life." Rory stared at his brother like he was comparing every detail.

Shiloh's forehead creased. "You knew about him and you're only just meeting now?"

Rory's dark eyes snapped to hers. "I was warned to stay away. If I'd come sooner, I would have jeopardized your fate. I had to wait until the time came."

"Time for what?" Dev asked.

"The time for retribution. Old cycles must end. The balance of power must be restored."

Shiloh folded her arms. The retribution? There wouldn't be one. Even if she died so Devlin could kill Jax. The cycle would start all over again. "What made you think it was happening now?"

And what the hell is taking Ren so long?

Rory's gaze probed hers and he gave her a sad smile. Had he heard her thoughts?

Rory's hand squeezed her shoulder before dropping to his side. "The woman who helped exhume my body and bring me back to life, she's a witch. She watches over us. She knew my parents. She knows about the prophecy. She saw what happened to Devlin's mam."

Maybe the witch had information that could turn their luck around.

Ren entered, carrying a lifeless Lanie in her arms.

Shiloh blinked, taking a minute to understand what she was seeing. The moment it registered, her heart staggered to a stop in her chest. "Noooo!" Shiloh screamed and ran to Lanie's side. Taking her sister's

body, Shiloh crumpled to the floor, rocking Lanie in her arms.

"Relax. I bit her," Ren drawled.

Shiloh's tear-soaked eyes speared the goth. "You, what?"

"I gotta go bury her. She'll be baked in a few weeks. Just chill."

"How can I chill? She's not sixteen yet. And, aren't you bonded? How can you exchange blood with anyone but Lock?"

"We're mates, but she won't accept my bond. And now I get why." Lock winked at Ren.

A silver-haired woman edged into the room, crouching at Shiloh's feet. "Shiloh. I'm Raine. Your sister wasn't going to make it. Evren saved her life." Raine's tentative touch rested on Shiloh's shoulder. "It was the only way. I'm sorry."

Silence descended, broken only by Shiloh's soft weeping. She touched her sister's face, recoiling at the chill kissing her pale skin.

"I gotta go bury her," Ren repeated.

Shiloh tightened her grip, feeling like a piece of her had been stolen.

"Allow me." Rory bent to her level, holding out his arms.

She sniffled, searching his gaze again for that tie. She'd known him before. She was sure of it. He looked down at her sister like she was precious. Irreplaceable.

Love was the only motive in his eyes. Nodding, Shiloh let him take her. Her empty arms went numb without their anchor.

Shiloh dragged her gaze away to take in her sister's savior. "Thank you, Evren."

"I told ya, don't mention it." She rolled her eyes before leaving the room.

"I'll see you soon, brother." Rory followed.

Devlin scooped Shiloh up off the ground, holding her close to his heart as he took her through the bunker to a bedroom.

He sat on the bed with her in his lap. "She'll be okay."

Her head rested on his shoulder, hand sliding to his chest to feel the beat beneath his ribcage. "What do we do now?"

"We're goin' to Scotland. We got a prophecy to hunt."

Chapter

Sixteen

Ancestors

Hand in hand, Shiloh and Devlin walked across the cobblestone road towards the Old Inn. Three stories of gothic history overlooked the grounds of Dunfermline Abbey. Black paint cloaked the ground floor façade, number thirteen mounted on a plaque over the entrance. *Mm, inviting.*

Walking inside, Shiloh was hit with the smell of greasy burgers, smoke, and beer. Pub music provided a background din. Lime green and purple covered the walls above wood panels. More timber created a grid on the ceiling, the color of the grain, deepened by years of exposure to the pub air, laden with toxins. Worn leather sofas lined the edges of the eating area.

She looked over the patrons, searching for the most likely candidate for a thousand-year-old witch. She found an elderly couple sitting in a studded leather booth, laughing hysterically over a shared joke.

"That's gotta be her." D tugged on Shiloh's hand.

A flawless redhead sat at the bar in a flowing floral dress and cardigan. Her head turned in their direction as she sipped from a highball glass.

"As I live and breathe, here you are, Devlin. You are so much like your brother." She put down her glass, spun on the stool, and offered her hand to Shiloh. "And your mistress. Shiloh, is it? What a beauty."

Shiloh took her hand, a jolt of electricity shooting up her arm. She yanked her hand away, giving it a shake.

"Airmid," Devlin confirmed.

"The one and only."

"Rory filled you in on why we're here?" Devlin raised a brow.

Airmid smiled, nodding. "I've been waiting for this meeting for a long time."

"Where can we go to talk?" Shiloh asked.

"Follow me." Airmid took them through a corridor to a narrow stairwell, the bells on her flip flops jingling. They ascended two levels to an apartment.

"After you." She waved them in.

The decor was an eclectic mix of old and new. Mismatched lamps, rugs, and cushions clashed with the green velvet sofa. Picture frames in every size and shape

crowded the walls. Rosemary, mint, and thyme infused the air with their fragrance.

"Have a seat. Would you like a herbal tea?"

"No. We ain't got time. We need to find this prophecy." Devlin shook his head, tugging Shiloh onto the green velvet seat. They sat side by side, hands refusing to release their hold.

"You *are* the prophecy, my dears." Airmid smiled as she folded elegantly into a purple paisley armchair, before crossing her legs.

We are the prophecy?

"What you really need, is to understand *who* threatens to take it from you. Do you know the story of your father?" She addressed Devlin.

"He was the first vampire. The virus started with him. I dunno how or why."

She tutted. "Your mother should've filled you in, but you were so young. She thought she was protecting you by hiding things, when in reality she did more damage than good." One manicured nail flicked a stray lock of hair to the side.

Circling a finger in the air, Airmid thrust her arm towards an old wireless and it powered up. Classic Billy Holiday lent a melody to their meeting. She tapped her ear, mouthing *they're listening*. Devlin's hand tightened on Shiloh's, pulling it into his lap.

Crossing the room, Airmid turned up the radio the old-fashioned way before returning. She didn't immediately sit. Stretching out her arm, she made an arc

in the air over them, a dome of protection forming along its path. The music faded, almost muting entirely as it closed over.

"There, that's better." Taking her seat, she crossed her legs again and smiled. "Your father was born in a time when the gods walked the Earth. He was jealous of their powers and immortality, and demanded they teach him their secrets." She tapped her fingers to the beat. "There were no secrets, of course. They were gods. They were created by a much higher force. The humans didn't like them and drove them back to the heavens. Jealous little creatures, they are.

"Before the gods left, he begged them to help him. What he didn't know was the being that offered its help was not a god, but a demon—Asmodeus, the Prince of Lust. He taught your father blood rituals that tainted his blood, causing the virus."

Airmid paused, walking to the window and checking the street. The bubble dome surrounding them warped and stretched to move with her, bouncing back when she returned. "Sorry, I thought I felt a presence." Clasping her hands, she perched herself on the edge of the chair. "It's a nasty affliction—bloodlust. Rumor is, he couldn't control it. He turned thousands of humans, discovering that siring vampires gave him control over them. He also found that vampires could still die from a mortal wound. Hunting down Asmodeus, your father demanded to be made immortal. The demon told him if he fathered a child with a Lilin, the child would cure his virus and provide him with immortality." She raised her clasped hands and pointed them at Devlin. "It achieved

both of those things. You cannot pass the virus on through a bite and your father will always live on through you. But that's not what he had in mind. He now seeks to destroy his creation, thinking that your power will be transferred to him."

"My father is dead."

"No, my dear. Jax is your father. He cannot be destroyed until you *bond* with your queen. Your brother has killed him many times, just as your father has killed your mate. You cannot be destroyed *once* you are bonded. He cannot be destroyed *until* you are bonded."

Shiloh met Devlin's hollow gaze, her stomach plummeting two stories to the inn below.

So that was it, then. They were officially screwed.

Devlin threw his head back, gulping down a shot of tequila in one go. He dropped the glass onto the table, spinning it in circles with only a filthy stare and invisible strings of energy. Shiloh felt the pulses bounce off the table and hit her in the chest. They were probably the only reason her heart kept beating. After their meeting with the witch upstairs, the organ had squeezed in her ribcage like it was trying to hide in a corner.

She sat across the booth in the inn, holding a shot of the Mexican spirit between her thumb and pointer finger. She'd never tasted tequila, but now seemed like a good time—with death breathing down her neck and all.

She raised the drink to her lips and poured it into her mouth. Swallowing, she smacked her lips.

Yeah, it burned.

I've endured worse.

The searing pain of bloodlust was infinitely more excruciating. Although, her craving had been satisfied after her flashback episode. She must've taken Jax's blood, somehow.

I guess I'll never know.

Any hope she'd harbored had been extinguished in the witch's apartment, three floors above the old inn. She only prayed that Lanie was going to be okay and that their parents would forgive her.

Mum, Dad, I'm sorry.

She wished she could say goodbye. Thank them for all they'd done for her.

Shiloh turned her attention to the windows, unable to see much through the smeared glass and smoky air. The woman who'd saved Devlin was buried here somewhere. She wondered if Devlin wanted to see Magaidh. He said he hadn't visited her grave since he'd moved to America.

I want to thank her.

"Where's your aunt buried?"

His power retreated, the rapping on her sternum ceasing its rhythm. The glass stopped spinning. His questioning gaze met hers. "Across the street, in the Abbey's yard."

"Can we? Would you be all right with seeing her?"

Pulling to his feet, he came to her side of the booth, reaching for her hand. "Yeah, babe. That's all good with me."

———

Dunfermline Abbey rose beyond the trees as they exited the inn. Its tower, declaring Robert the Bruce as its eternal king, topped the imposing medieval stone relic. Devlin scanned the shadows for any threats, flaring his nostrils to catch any whiff of ambush as they entered the grounds. Rounding the south side of the building, they picked their way through the headstones to the southwest corner of the churchyard. The frosty air nipped at the back of his neck as he lit a cigarette, clouds of smoke blending with the mists and the ghostly occupants roaming the night.

"They're over here." Buried with kings and saints. As it should be for the woman who'd saved him, and her stillborn son.

He survived. Devlin hadn't really believed the story his brother had spilled until he'd met the witch who'd helped dig Rory out.

Shiloh didn't wait for Devlin's direction. She beelined straight to the grave like she'd been the one to lay them to rest.

"Here," she whispered.

A Celtic cross of stone marked the grave. No names. No dates.

Devlin wasn't even sure why he'd chosen to keep them a secret. *How'd she know where they were?*

"Yeah." His voice croaked. The tequila should've melted the icicles from his vocal chords, but it hadn't.

"I feel her."

Magaidh was Shiloh's ancestor. Of course she knew where to find her.

In a deafening roar, the earth rumbled under their feet. It was a moment's warning before a cavity yawned above the grave. Two skeletal hands latched onto Shiloh's ankles and pulled her in. Landslides of soil immediately cut off her scream, the grave presenting a dormant facade, mocking Devlin's frantic attempts to carve under its surface.

"No! Shiloh!" He clawed at the earth, his fingernails ripping as they met the unyielding ground. It was like the soil had fossilized.

Lurching to his feet, he thrust out his arms, his fingers stretched. Breath sawing, heart thundering, he concentrated his power down to the bleeding tips of his fingers. Waves of energy pummeled the earth.

"Oomph." The force ricocheted back at him, knocking him on his ass and stealing his breath.

He groaned, pain shooting up his spine and into his skull. *Fuck.* He told his legs to bend, but they scissored lamely. He was like a boxer trying to come back after a KO. Between his ears, the ringer was turned to full volume. Above him, the scattering of stars smudged as his vision checked in and out.

I gotta get up. Gotta get her back.

He tried again, this time ordering his torso off the ground. The grunt he made was a joke considering he didn't move more than an inch.

His eyelids peeled wide as the ground rumbled again. Shiloh burst into the air, dirt spraying everywhere. She hovered above his fallen form, her eyes glowing icy white. With her hair floating around her in an inky mist, she looked possessed. Her mouth opened, worms slithering out and falling on his face. He shook his head, dislodging their slimy bodies.

Words chased the worms' retreat, spilling from her mouth in Magaidh's voice:

Once man reaches beyond his heights,

And gods engage in sinister rites.

A plague upon humankind does blight,

Death consumes by bloodlust's bite.

Heaven's wrath courts the forsaken,

Demons and angels, pleasures partaken.

The retribution birthed at daybreak,

A mother's love burned at the stake.

Heaven and hell unite with creation,

New flesh revived in brilliant salvation.

The light extinguished behind Shiloh's eyes before she dropped on top of him like a stone.

His arms flung around her. "Shiloh! Fuck. No." Giving her a gentle shake, he pressed two fingers on the side of her neck in search of a pulse. The only heartbeat he felt was his own rattling his brain.

I'm not letting you go. This ain't over, goddamn it.

He rolled her, placing her back onto the grass. Pinching her nose and covering her mouth with his, he blew air into her lungs. "Come on, Shiloh."

He felt for her pulse again. Nothing.

Starting chest compressions, he counted aloud. Anything to distract him from the images flashing across his mind. He'd never met his grandfather and he sure as fuck didn't want a visit from the sickle-wielding, robe-wearing angel of death now.

Rory slammed onto the ground beside him. "I'll do compressions. You breathe for her."

Shouldering Devlin out of the way, his brother pumped on her chest, forcing her heart to move. Dev covered her mouth again, her chest rising only a little under the force of Rory's compressions. He stopped and pressed two fingers to her neck. Frowning, he continued to massage her heart.

"Magaidh!" Airmid bellowed from yards away.

She must've been watching through her window above the inn.

The brothers fell back onto the grass, knocked back by the glowing misty form of Magaidh as she rose from her grave. She swooped down into Shiloh's body, like she'd been sucked in by a vacuum. Shiloh lifted a few feet off the ground, her body bowing backwards. Dragging in a great suck of air, her eyes sprung open. She coiled into a ball before collapsing to the earth, panting.

Magaidh's mist drifted out and dissipated away.

Devlin reached for Shiloh, wrapping her legs and arms around him so he could hold her. "You still with me?"

Her chin pressed into his neck. "Mm."

Thank fuck.

She was alive. Shaking like a junky, but alive. His head swiveled back to Airmid. The witch nodded with a smile before leaving them there.

Rory stood, clapping palms with his brother and pulling the pair upright.

"Welcome back, brother. This is how we roll in the old country."

Fucking God bless America.

Chapter

Seventeen

Well Played, Asshole

Nestled in the hills east of Oxton, Rory's cottage posed a lonely figure on the rolling green landscape. Dark clouds shaded the terrain and denied them the sun's warmth. Devlin swung an axe, splitting a block of wood, and threw the pieces into a wheelbarrow. He grabbed another and placed it on the tree stump.

The cottage was in a perfect spot. The hills protected its back. There were open views of the valley in front of them. There was no way they wouldn't see any mofos coming. They were prepped and ready. The little house didn't look like much on the surface, but that shit was an iceberg. Above ground, it was all *Better Homes and Gardens*. Down below, he had a whole level

dedicated to weapons. Below that, another level for combat training and strategic planning. Below that, he had a fucking panic room.

Damn, Devlin was tempted to camp out in there. Beneath his cool exterior, he was shitting himself.

Looking in through the windows, he caught sight of Shiloh sitting in front of the fire. A blanket covered her shoulders and her hands curled around a mug of steaming tea in her lap. Her head lolled to the side. Margo came into view, rescuing the tea before it spilled.

The ground steadied under his feet and his jaw loosened a little. His second in command had his back. Always. He needed something? She made it happen. She'd seen him lose his shit two hundred years ago in San Jose. She'd given him space to grieve. Then she'd knocked him the fuck out and told him to find his balls.

And here he was, faced with losing his mate again. He didn't know if it was better to have the warning, or to have her life ripped away suddenly. His brows pulled together, a pain throbbing in his chest. Her body was failing. All the sleeping, the mood swings, not wanting to eat—she was shutting down.

Jax's baby grew inside her, sucking her life-force dry.

Even without the pregnancy, he'd seen this pattern too many times. Sadistic motherfuckers like Jax had been crawling out of their graves and into any pair of unsuspecting panties they could find for centuries. They all wanted one thing: power. They spun lust into

something resembling love so they could own the blood of their victims.

It stank of Asmodeus, Prince of Lust. Devlin's father wasn't the only one doing the work of the demon. The entity preyed on the ones who thought they had their shit together. Not the ones who knew their weaknesses. No. Because if you knew your issues you were already aware enough to guard against their exploitation. Chances were, you were working on cutting the crap. But Asmodeus enabled his victims to swallow their own bullshit and ask for seconds.

Maybe Shiloh had been vulnerable 'cause she'd thought she was invincible. But he didn't buy it. This was different. This dispute was centuries in the making. She'd had a target on her head before she was conceived.

He swung the axe, the crack reverberating off the hillside. Tossing the tool in with the wood, he wheeled it to the mudroom entrance.

Rory met him at the door. "Thanks, brother."

"Did she fall asleep again?" Removing his jacket, Devlin hung it on a hook.

"Margo just tucked her in."

"Can you promise me somethin'?"

"Aye."

"If I die before I get to kill him, you gotta put him in the ground for me."

"Done."

He didn't need to ask. His brother's sword had spilled their father's blood before. But Devlin still gripped onto the hope that the cycle would finally end, by the tips of his fingernails.

The brothers joined the rest of the team in the living room, wood smoke a comforting companion.

"Have you been able to contact Carter?" Lock threw out the question.

"Nada." And Devlin didn't fucking like it, at all.

His intestines twisted up through his body and wrapped around his heart. No. She wouldn't dare to go against him. Sienna knew what he was capable of.

Or would she?

Sienna had been responsible for protecting Lanie while she'd been in hospital. And the cop had put Shiloh's parents in a safe house.

Fuck. Devlin's chest just about caved in.

"You want me to—" Lock started to ask.

"Car approaching," Ren butted in from her station at the window.

Devlin and Rory crossed the room to peer over her shoulder.

"Pass me the binoculars." Dev held his hand out to Margo, who'd claimed the other narrow window at the front.

"Here." She hooked the strap over his palm. "Looks like Sienna, but she's not alone."

"She didn't tell us she was coming. I smell a fucking rat," Ren snarled.

"It's Sienna. Myles is in the passenger seat. Looks like the kid is in the back, too."

Why the fuck would Zain and Myles be in Scotland?

Why would Carter?

Sienna had to be on the ground in LA. Besides, her job didn't permit her to travel unless it was for personal reasons.

Maybe this is personal?

Why the fuck else would she be halfway across the world?

None of them had a reason to be here. And they hadn't cleared it with him.

"Suit up. They ain't gettin' in." He handed the binoculars back to Margo.

"Want me to get the bazooka?"

Tempting. This was why he kept her around. No questions asked. Ready to fuck shit up at any time.

"No. I wanna hear the excuse before their heads roll. Get Shiloh to safety."

Margo clapped her hands and trotted towards the bedrooms, pulling to a stop when her path was blocked.

"What's going on?" Shiloh shuffled into the room, bleary-eyed.

"We got company," Devlin answered.

She stepped up to his side. "Who?"

"Hollywood is in town, but they ain't got no business here."

"Hollywood?" Her brows pulled together.

"The doc, the kid, and the cop."

Outside, the car pulled to a stop and four car doors slammed.

Four.

"Aw, fuck. Well played, asshole," Ren spat.

Devlin leaned over, peering through the blinds. "Fuck!" he roared, pulling Shiloh into his chest and shielding her eyes. "Get her to the panic room, now!"

No. Not her parents. *Motherfucking bastard.*

Margo reached for Shiloh's shoulders, her palms rebounding off thin air as Devlin's hold was wrenched away and he slid back two feet. Shiloh tipped up her face, black gaze honing in on him. "Let me go."

The door shook on its hinges, a trio of thumps pounding its surface. "Shiloh, I brought you a present." Jax's voice seeped under the barrier.

She stepped towards the door.

"Don't—" Devlin reached for her, his hand hitting resistance that stung. *Shit.* He ignored the excruciating pain burning through his skin, desperate to break through the surface. She knocked him back. Rory came at her, recoiling with a hiss as his hands slipped off the biting air. Nobody could touch her. He hoped to fuck Jax wouldn't be able to either.

She opened the door, eyelids peeling back, mouth levering wide. Her scream pierced the air until it rippled, windows shattering and the car alarm blaring in symphony. *Fuck.* She should never have had to witness the sight of her parents' bloodied, lifeless bodies stuffed into the fucking boot of a car. Necks gaping, their eyes stared blankly at nothing. His hands gripped fistfuls of his hair. The sight of her agony carved into his bones with a hatchet.

Releasing a feral snarl, anger lit a furnace in his soul. Why couldn't he reverse time to the point before his father was born? The gods responsible for dishing out this fate needed to be gutted.

Devlin walked around Shiloh's frozen form and down the steps. Bloodied, bruised, bound, and gagged, Zain and Myles kneeled beside the open boot. Sienna and Jax stood behind them, the barrels of their guns pressed to their prisoners' heads.

"Zain," Shiloh cried.

Devlin's team formed a perimeter around the scene, weapons cocked. Rory stood to his left, sword gripped in hand. Margo flanked his right, staring down the barrel of her shotgun, Jax in her sight. Lock emptied his magazine into the hood of the car, silencing the alarm before reloading. Ren twirled her daggers in her hands, black-rimmed eyes fixed on the back of Margo's head.

Devlin stared Sienna down. She returned his gaze with malevolence. *Fucking bitch.* His fangs punched out, his muscles damn near ripping from his bones with the need to tear her in half. He twisted his neck, cracking the vertebrae into alignment. As he raised a clawed hand, it

pulsed with his hatred. The picture of her spine snapping, clear as crystal in his head, translated to reality. The snap sounded before her body collapsed on the gravel.

Beside him, Margo snorted. Ren lifted one corner of her lips, switching her gaze to Jax as she continued her party trick.

Devlin had hoped to feel satisfaction.

He didn't feel a fucking thing.

Jax gave him an ovation. "Impressive. She'd served her purpose." Turning to Shiloh, he added, "You didn't think you found the exit by chance, did you? Your boyfriend has done me a favor."

Devlin eyeballed his father through blazing lenses, his heart a block of stone in his chest.

"Give me Shiloh and I'll give her parents a proper burial and rebirth. I'll even throw in a couple of freebies." He booted Zain in the head, crushing his skull.

The crack made Devlin's neck prickle. The kid's body slumped, his chest deflating with his last exhale. Shiloh screamed again.

"Oh, dear. Make that one freebie."

Devlin's boot crunched the gravel as he twisted his heel, a lion preparing to pounce. Behind him, Shiloh wailed, "Stop. Please, stop."

"Is it true that I'm going to be a papa?" Jax's arms spread wide before Shiloh's body slammed into his like an elastic snapping back in place.

Devlin lurched for her but ricocheted off her protective bubble.

Jax is immune to her defenses? The bond. Goddamn it.

Spinning her in his arms, Jax's filthy hands caressed the tiny bump of her belly. "Ah, there you are."

She tried turning away, sucking in breaths through gritted teeth. "Don't touch me."

One hand slid between her legs. She writhed, a mask of terror slipping into place. "You used to beg for my touch. You loved my cock pumping into your pussy, dirty little whore." He licked his lips, sniffing her neck. "All Lilith's children love to fuck. Lanie was no exception. At least she made things more of a challenge—something you never did." He pulled her hair off her neck. "Always such a good girl. Always doing what you're told. It was so easy to lure you in, I barely had to do anything. Were you so starved of affection?" Jax's head warped between looking like a ram and a bull before returning to normal. "Or did you need to be a bad girl for a change, huh?"

Ren's blade flew through the air, missing Jax's head by an inch and lodging in the wall of the cottage behind Devlin.

"Ren!" he barked.

"Sorry. I slipped." She shrugged.

Jax snapped his teeth near Shiloh's ear, eyes narrowing on Devlin. "Keep your pets in check." His

gaze slid to Shiloh's pulsing neck. "I don't want the mother of my child injured."

He dragged in a breath through his nose. "Mm. Maybe I should've kept Lanie as a plaything like I did with Magaidh." He tutted. "Such a pity. Her blood served its purpose. The blood of his ancestors." He nodded towards Devlin. "I learned that little spell from Magaidh the night I killed her sister. You know, the stake where she burned is still there. Would you like to see it?" he asked Shiloh.

Her face smoothed in a serene mask of surrender. Her eyes lifted to Devlin as she mouthed, *I love you.* Pulling one arm out from Jax's embrace, she aimed a finger at Rory. The sword whipped from his palm and speared straight through Jax's hands, plunging into Shiloh's womb. Her body folded forward, Jax's gargled cry following her down. He yanked his hands away, pulling out the sword, and bolted.

Devlin was by her side in one leap, yelling at his team, "Don't kill him. He still has a part of her soul."

Lock and Ren kicked up dust as they took off.

Rory scooped his sword off the ground, his wings busting out and tearing off his shirt. "I'll keep him breathing. That's all I'm promising." He bent powerful legs before thrusting into the air.

Devlin's hands pressed into Shiloh's stomach, blood pumping out from beneath his fingers. Her face drained of color as he watched a crimson pond forming. Her eyes rolled. Body quaking, she fought for breath. He

clenched his teeth; his brow scrunched. He purged his grief in anguished groans.

Margo ran from the cottage, a wad of fabric in her hands. She pushed it onto his hands, grabbing his wrists and guiding his palms into place on top of Shiloh's stomach.

"It's too late," Devlin croaked.

"No, it's not!" she barked. "Press harder."

His hands went limp. Margo jumped into place, taking over. "Give her your blood."

And speed things up? "I can't."

"Why? How much more damage do you think you can do? Give her your blood; it's her only chance!"

He jumped to his feet. Spinning around, he raced up the steps and ripped the knife from the wall. Leaping back to Shiloh's side, he slashed his wrists lengthwise and held them over her gasping mouth.

She gargled and choked. Margo propped Shiloh's shoulders up on one knee while leaning over to keep the pressure on the wound.

Within seconds, her gargles turned to gulps. Her hands grasped at his wrists, holding them in place.

It's working. Thank fuck.

The pressure in his chest eased.

Spots of white bleached his vision as his pulse slowed.

Take it, babe. Take it all.

His body numbed, his bulk slumping to the side.

"Devlin?" Margo's voice traveled down a long tunnel.

"Dev—"

Chapter Eighteen

The Seal

Shiloh's brain came back online, tuning in to her surroundings. *What's that smell? Burning flesh?* Eyes focusing, she watched embers and flames rise from a bonfire. Lock and Ren collected dead bodies from the field, adding more fuel. *What the hell happened?*

More senses came online. Her hands were locked around someone's wrists, her chin sticky, and the taste of heaven on her tongue. Her torso shunted sideways as something shoved her. Looking left she saw Margo, tears streaming down her face. Her palms dropped from Shiloh's shoulders, gaze sliding down.

Sucking in a breath, horror stole Shiloh's voice.

Devlin. Dropping his wrists, she scrambled to her knees, bending over his cold body.

"You drank him dry," Margo cried.

No. Shiloh rejected the explanation, her hair whipping about as she shook her head.

The blue-haired warrior sniffed, scrubbing at her face. "He's been dead for an hour. I couldn't get near you to wake you up."

Dragging him into her lap, Shiloh curled herself around him.

No. No. No.

She buried her face in his hair.

The sound of laughter registered, her gaze swiveling behind her to the source. Jax. What kind of sick fucking joke was this?

Devlin's brother stood over him, boot planted in his back and sword poised at the nape of Jax's neck. "Say the word," Rory gritted out.

Hovering over the brother, the ghosts of Magaidh and her sister shimmered in the air. Slowly shaking their heads in tandem, they warned Shiloh against taking Rory's offer.

Holding Devlin's head in her lap, she pleaded with them. "Help. Please?"

Magaidh's misty form collapsed into a ball of light, shooting up into the sky to join the stars. *Please, please, please. Help.* Shiloh was supposed to die, not him. *Devlin. God.* She'd been the one to kill him. *How could I have done this?*

She sucked in shallow breaths. Anything to fill the empty void behind her ribs. She wondered if her soul

had gone with his, leaving nothing but a buzz of pain and guilt to torture her. How was it possible that her body hadn't imploded into the vacuum?

Devlin's mother came down to kneel beside her fallen son.

"I'm so s-sorry," Shiloh sobbed.

Forming a semicircle around them, Devlin's team stood, heads bowed, faces slack. Rory hadn't budged in his stance, still aiming his sharp tip of steel at the vampire from hell. He should be aiming his blade at her.

It wasn't meant to end like this.

Dev's mam smiled, stroking a palm down Shiloh's face before pointing into the distance. A ball of light flashed on the crest of the hill, rolling down the slope and growing larger as it gained ground. Closing the distance, it took shape.

Airmid.

Magaidh had brought the witch.

"No. You fucking bi—" Jax's growl cut off as the tip of Rory's sword nicked his neck.

Rory's scowl turned into a cocky smile as he stared down at his prisoner. "You can do nothing now. Fate is unavoidable. The light will always win. Ladies and gentlemen, I give you *the* witch."

Margo clapped her hands. "Ooh, you're screwed now, buddy. This is gonna be so good! Fuck, where's the popcorn?"

"The witch is here?" Lock whistled, his stance straightening. "Got any marshmallows?"

"We can roast them on the bonfire." Ren's eyes flashed at her mate.

Airmid stopped a few yards away, nodding at Shiloh. Holding an arm out to one side, she skipped in a circle, her arm forming the radius, her hand in the center. She stood back and sang a Gaelic chant. The power she emanated skittered over Shiloh's skin. Within the circle, the earth danced to her rhythm, a deep hole carving itself into the ground.

Airmid came to Shiloh. "Give him to me, child."

Shiloh unwrapped her arms and legs. Her body swayed forward as Devlin's weight was lifted from her. She didn't want to let go.

"It's okay." The witch smiled and turned her attention to Magaidh. "If you would be so kind?"

His aunt's misty form nodded, enveloping their bodies. She lifted them up and plunged them into the hole.

"What is she doing?" Shiloh struggled to her feet.

"Bathing him in the Well of Sláine. Airmid has the power to revive the dead," Rory answered.

Power pulsed under her sternum before spreading out to her extremities. The vacuum inside her was filled with a pressure so great, she wondered if she might explode. *Devlin. He's going to come back to me.*

Shiloh peered into the well. It presented a dark abyss. The kind of place you'd expect to welcome death, not restore life. She waited, chewing on her lips. All she could do was trust, hope, and pray.

Airmid's voice echoed from the void. "She is free of him. Your blood has burned away all traces of him in her veins. You *must* seal your bond and return her soul."

A howling wind chased her words, as if a storm barreled from the bowels of the Earth. Shiloh backed away, her mouth going dry while her pulse thundered.

"Welcome to the retribution, motherfucker." Rory put more weight behind his boot. Jax's grunt drew a smirk on D's brother's face.

On a gush of wind, Devlin rocketed from the well. His wings spread wide in an impressive display. Cheers rose from the crowd. Shiloh took in his brilliance, her heart squeezing in her chest. Happy tears wet her cheeks, her smile splitting her face. His eyes glowed, shooting beams of light as they locked on to Shiloh.

I would have you in a second. Come at me with all you've got; I can take it.

Swooping down, he gathered her in his arms and whisked her away. His fangs struck at her throat, shooting a bolt of pleasure to her core. *Yes.* Pressing her chest into his, her hands hooked under his arms. Walking her fingers up, she touched the soft feathers of his wings, feeling him twitch in response. He groaned and pressed his hips into hers. Every nerve ending was lit up. Her pulse sped along, giving him the nourishment he craved.

She wanted to feel him inside her for their bodies to reach new heights of pleasure.

She set her wings free, pulling the two of them higher and higher, the cottage shrinking to a speck way below. Fumbling with the zipper of his jeans, she eased it down and reached inside to find him ready to go. The wind whipped around them, its freezing caress no match for their twin flames.

He retracted his fangs, setting free a satisfied sigh. Licking her neck before kissing a trail to her mouth, he groaned, "Fuck. I gotta have you."

Her heart stuttered, core clenching. *Yes, please.*

He tore off her jeans, letting them fall. Diving his hand into her panties, he ran his fingers along her slick heat. Her body jerked, her wings shuddering as pleasure flooded her senses.

Pulling the cotton aside, she lined up his cock and urged him to plunge in deep. She sucked in a breath, her fingers digging into his waist. *Oh, yes, holy mother of God.* The way he stretched her was delicious. Their union unlocked the last piece she'd been missing. This was completion.

Sparks of electricity trailed the drag of skin on skin, their bites heightening every sensation. The lovers' hips pumped in sync. She didn't know if they were still flying, or plummeting to the ground. She couldn't have cared less. In tasting his kiss, pressing into his flesh, being surrounded by his arms, there was only heaven.

The pair's combined power snowballed and twirled. She moaned. A touch of fear that it was too

much merged with her pleasure. A force rushed up and down their bodies, penetrating deep from one to the other before arcing out in a field around them. It was their bond. It had to be. Nothing else could be that powerful. They were a supernova, ready to blow. Their skin began to glimmer, blinding light flashing as their ecstasy hit a pinnacle. Devlin released a long groan, Shiloh delivering a cry in harmony. A moment of weightlessness suspended them before they shuddered in unison. The two, bonded as one.

Still gripping each other, gravity tipped them over, dragging them headfirst to the ground. Devlin spread his wings, gliding through the sky. "Fucking, finally." He pressed his lips hard onto hers. "I don't wanna pull out. Can I stay inside forever?"

She laughed, placing her forehead on his chest. She didn't want him to go either. But way below them, they'd left things undone. "No. I've got shit to do." She squeezed him on the butt before pushing him away. Tumbling through the air, she straightened her panties. Flapping her wings, she steadied her path. Devlin glided in beside her, a grin on his face.

She twisted her lips to the side to stop herself mirroring his expression. "I don't mean to kill the vibe, but we've got to deal with your father."

His grin merged into a perverse smile. "I'm looking forward to it."

Chapter

Nineteen

I'll Take That, Thanks.

Boom. Devlin landed, forming a small crater in the field beside the cottage. The bond between them hummed. The burden he'd carried his entire life had extinguished the moment he and Shiloh had lit up the sky. He was ready to end this for real.

He stalked over to his brother. The guy hadn't dropped his guard, sword still ready to plunge. Devlin was damn lucky to have Rory on his side.

Jax had one eye fixed on Devlin with the other pressed into the gravel. "Have fun?"

Devlin's hand snapped out and sent a crushing force down onto his father's head. The asshole screamed like a bitch. *Just one more pulse . . .*

"Wait." Shiloh exited the cottage wearing clean clothes and joined them. "He has something of mine. I want it back."

Could he tap into the ability his grandfather possessed now that his power had been freed? Airmid had said *'return her soul'*. He'd damn sure try. "It'd be my pleasure to get it from him." He tossed his chin at Rory. "Flip him over, brother."

Rory obliged, stomping his foot on Jax's stomach and holding the sword at his neck.

Crouching down, Devlin rubbed his palms together. Drawing on the heat until his hands glowed, he placed them on his father's chest.

His eyelids dropped. He'd never done this before, but something told him this was what he was meant to do. This was the tool he'd been given in order to fulfill his destiny as the savior of the human race. All those sons of bitches stealing souls—they were fucked now.

He focused on Shiloh's unique vibration, calling it out of his father. He pulled. And he pulled. He yanked the missing piece of her soul right out of Jax's chest. His father howled in pain. Holding the ball of light in his hand, Devlin walked to his mate.

Pressing the orb over her heart, he watched it disappear.

A soft sigh escaped, her eyes sparking with fireworks. Shiloh swayed towards him. "Thank you." She pressed a kiss to his lips.

Backing away, she blew out a breath before inky black eclipsed the whites of her eyes. Her jaw jutted out and set in stone, eyebrows slamming down. She leaned forward, facing Jax.

He writhed, dislodged Rory's boot, and sprang to his feet.

Shiloh thrust out her arm, her palm facing the demon. He froze, unable to move.

Devlin's mouth fell open as he watched Shiloh's skin dissolve, her body taking liquid form. Blood. She was pure blood. Like a tsunami hitting the shore, she rushed towards Jax, swirling around his body before pouring her entire being down his throat.

Shiloh! Jesus.

What the hell? Had Devlin lost her again?

He stumbled a few steps, not knowing whether to cut the bastard open and get her back, or just trust that she knew what she was doing.

Jax seized, choking like his airways had been obstructed, cutting off his oxygen. Hands grabbing at his neck and chest, he fell to his knees before abruptly catapulting into the air. His arms flung wide, legs stiffening. His eyelids peeled back as his eyeballs rolled. The skin and flesh ripped from his body, exploding in a bloody downpour. Black vapor plumed from the carnage, collecting in a cloud, and barreled off over the hills.

Where Jax had been, Shiloh took form once more.

Holy fucking shit. What just happened?

Devlin swayed on his feet. Covered in the splattered remains of his father, his stomach threatened to do the bolt.

"He's dead. It's done. But I couldn't destroy the demon." Shiloh set her feet back on solid ground. Her body was drenched in Jax's blood.

Asmodeus. He escaped. *Goddamnit.*

"Oh, man. The stench." Margo wiped the hem of her shirt across her face.

Lock's eyes glazed. "That shit is gonna give me nightmares for fucking eons."

"Where's the bleach?" Ren pinched her shirt, pulling it away from her body.

Rory headed towards the house. "Use the mudroom entrance. I'll not have that filth in my house. And don't forget you've got a prisoner in the panic room."

What?

"Myles." Ren answered his unspoken question. "We can't trust him now."

"Where are Magaidh and Airmid? And Devlin's mother?" Shiloh asked, her hands twisting together as she searched the terrain.

"The sisters took the witch back. Don't worry, we thanked them for you. You can catch 'em up later."

Margo winked. She trailed behind the team as they set off after his brother, Rory saying something about a hose down.

Shiloh didn't follow, her gaze finding the abandoned car instead. Folding her arms, she returned to the horror scene in the boot. Zain's body lay only a foot away.

Devlin followed his mate, the sight of her dead parents still a kick in the gut.

He carefully lifted them out and placed the bodies on the grass.

Pulling one of Shiloh's hands into his, he squeezed it. "We'll do right by them."

"I didn't want this life for my parents. They wouldn't have survived in this world."

"It ain't for everyone."

If he had to choose between this life, or living without her, he'd choose her. Every time.

"Do you think Lanie will be okay?"

"Babe, Lanie is tougher than titanium. Do you think she gives a shit if she was bitten a little early? Fuck, no. She'll do what she damn well wants. The virus don't stand a chance."

"I hope you're right."

"I got a feelin' she's gonna do big things."

Devlin eyed his brother's sword, lying on the ground. He'd better do right by her. *Pfft*. Who was Devlin kidding? In the short time he'd known him, Rory

had shown more honor than anyone Devlin had met. Lanie was damn lucky. But Rory? The poor bastard was in for a world of pain.

She is gonna kick your ass, brother.

To be continued . . .

Read on for a sneak peek at Bone and Blood . . .

Bone

and

Blood

Prologue

Rory squatted atop a rocky outcrop, looking at the ground below. The quarry just north of Los Angeles was a mecca for vampires needing to bury their freshly drained victims. The scent of their kind soaked the air. He'd been perched on the hill for two days and he'd witnessed five newborns crawling from their graves. Not his mate, though. Not yet.

He took a swig from his bottle and sniffed, trying to pick out her fragrance. The December sky presented a crisp blue canvas. He wasn't yet accustomed to the

sunshine in this part of the world. His skin had turned a darker shade of brown, making his tattoo a little less obvious. He did not miss the snow. *I could get used to this.*

His nose twitched. *Was that . . .?* He pulled to his feet, his gaze fixed on her grave. Had it changed shape? Was there any hint of a fingernail or nose reaching for the light?

His head jerked back as the grave blew open, his mate leaping onto her feet.

Whoa. She's incredible.

Not a bit of her was free of dust. Her hair resembled a nest atop her head, but Rory didn't care about any of that. He cared about the determined way she scrambled up to the ridge where he waited, and the intelligent light in her eye as she sized him up.

"Who—" She coughed out puffs of quarry dust. "Ugh, fuck." Spitting on the ground, she aimed her stare at him once more. "Who the fuck are you?"

He bowed. "Rory Vice. I'm your mate."

Pulling her head back, her eyebrows creased, eyes popping wide.

"I thought you might need some assistance."

"You got the wrong girl, buddy." She turned in a circle, looking out over the landscape before stomping off to the east.

"Might I make a suggestion?"

"Nope." She kept walking, occasionally stumbling on her newborn legs.

He grinned. She was entertaining, at the very least.

Pulling off his shirt, he tucked it into the waistband of his jeans, and shoved his drink bottle in his back pocket. His wings stretched out, capturing her in their shadow. Lifting off, he flew above her, landing in her path.

"What the frick?" She fell on her side, sliding down the ridge. "Ow, ow, ow." She hissed, shaking off grazed palms, and rubbing her thigh.

He kept his distance, not wanting to scare her any more than he already had. "I'm sorry. I was only trying to prevent wasted effort on your part."

"W-what are you?" Her irises had turned red.

"It'll take some explaining to answer that. May I offer you a ride?"

"A ride? Where's your passenger seat?" Her eyes flicked to his chest. Likely, his tattoo had captured her attention.

He spread his arms. "These are the only option."

He watched her throat bob. *She must be thirsty.*

"You don't know where I'm going."

"On the contrary. I can take you directly to where you need to go. Or, more importantly, to whom you need to see."

"And who's that?" Her eyes narrowed.

"Your sire, little vampire. You need your first feed."

———

Titles

by

J.M. Adele

Coming Home Series

Shattered Home

Remembering Home

Finding Home

Leaving Home (TBA)

Coming Home (TBA)

Sensing Series

Sensing You
Convincing You (2019)
Indulging You (TBA)

Bloodlust Series

Ashes and Dust
Ember and Flame
Bone and Blood (TBA)

Acknowledgements

I would sincerely like to thank all my readers who patiently waited for me to get my shit together so I could write this book. As most of you know, life is a juggling act. Parenthood, day job, business, writing, friends, family, self-care - do you see what I did there? Self-care came last. Yeah, that's how I lived my life. And it came back to bite me on the arse. I'm learning to fill my cup first before I play bartender to everyone else. Don't get me wrong, writing is my jam. But when everything else is pressing in, the jam oozes from the sandwich, and drips on the floor. Ugh. The crap that pours out when I haven't been kind to me isn't worth a damn. So, be kind to you.

I have to give a special mention to my betas and ARC readers. This book is dedicated to you because you waited so long and were so very important in making this book way better than what I could do on my own. Thank you so much!

To my beautiful Gems—my reader group—you are the fruit to my jam; so sweet, I just want to squish you! Enough said. ;P

To Anna and Lauren—damn, you ladies are good editors. I'm so lucky to have found you. And incredibly fortunate that you continue to put up with me. Many thanks.

Fiona! You squeezed my unorganized self in at the last minute, again! Thank you so much for being awesome! Romancing the Coast rocked, by the way. I think I might've mentioned it a couple of times. ;)

To Katja—I think I'm at 1000 IOU's. I so appreciate you. You deserve all the happiness in the world, my friend. I will never walk into a creepy forest at night thanks to you. O.o

To Jane—you're just as weird as me, and I love it. Thank you for adopting me and answering my S.O.S.

My beautiful Shell, you are the best of the best, always unfailing in your encouragement and support. You're a huge blessing in my life—never doubt that.

Robyn C.—I don't know how you do it, but I cannot thank you enough for your Facebook awesomeness. I'm in awe.

To Vicky—thanks for signing up for my craziness. I hope you don't regret it!

There are so many more . . .

To all the beautiful people whom I've met somewhere along this journey, you've changed me in ways you can't imagine. Thank you. For the love and for the lessons. It's all part of the plan. I get it now. I just hope you know who you are. I couldn't have done this without your support. Bear hugs to you all.

I left the most precious people until last. My boys. You are the best. When you ignore me, you are still the best. When you make me late for work, you're still the best. When you don't put your dirty washing in the basket, you're still the best. I will love you for eternity: it doesn't matter what you do, or don't do. I'm here for you always. xxxxxxxxxxxxxxxxxxxxxxxxxx

THAAANNNNK YOOOOOOUUU!

About

the

Author

Author of smart, sexy heroes, and heroines with brains and backbone; J.M. Adele loves to flit between the dark and light sides of romance.

She lives in Queensland with her three children and an almost constant procession of imaginary characters. Somewhere along the way they moved in and she went with it.

Her greatest joys are her boys, and her books.

Her biggest challenges are balancing wanderlust with the tendency to be a homebody, and battling an addiction to reading.

Not bad. Not bad at all.

Follow J.M.

Links to my newsletter and my Facebook reader group
can be found on my website.

     www.jmadele.com

     www.facebook.com/authorjmadele

     @JMAdeleBooks

     @j.m.adele